HOLLYWOOD HOLDUP

HOLLYWOOD HOLDUP

TYNDALE HOUSE PUBLISHERS, INC., CAROL STREAM, ILLINOIS

RED ROCK MYSTERIES

#1 BEST-SELLING AUTHORS

JERRY B. JENKINS · CHRIS FABRY

Visit Tyndale's exciting Web site for kids at cool2read.com
Also see the Web site for adults at tyndale.com

TYNDALE is a registered trademark of Tyndale House Publishers, Inc.
Tyndale Kids logo is a trademark of Tyndale House Publishers, Inc.

Hollywood Holdup

Designed by Jacqueline L. Noe
Edited by Lorie Popp

Published in association with the literary agency of Alive Communications, Inc., 7680 Goddard Street, Suite 200, Colorado Springs, CO 80920.

Library of Congress Cataloging-in-Publication Data
Jenkins, Jerry B.
   Hollywood holdup / Jerry B. Jenkins, Chris Fabry.
      p. cm. — (Red Rock mysteries ; 12)
   Summary: At Halloween, facing a series of disasters while pet sitting, thirteen-year-old twins Ashley and Bryce gain insights into their principal and classmate Boo, and investigate a string of robberies at fast food restaurants in and around Red Rock.
   ISBN-13: 978-1-4143-0151-8 (sc)
   ISBN-10: 1-4143-0151-0 (sc)
   [1. Pet sitting—Fiction. 2. Halloween—Fiction. 3. Stealing—Fiction. 4. Twins—Fiction. 5. Christian life—Fiction. 6. Mystery and detective stories. 7. Colorado—Fiction.] I. Fabry, Chris, 1961- . II. Title. III. Series: Jenkins, Jerry B. Red Rock mysteries ; 12.
   PZ7.J4138Hol 2006
   [Fic]—dc22   2005030286

Printed in the United States of America

09 08 07 06
9 8 7 6 5 4 3 2 1

*For the Middletons, especially Alyssa and Jesse,
with thanks to Kelli for her drive-thru stories*

"I know a dead parrot when I see one, and I'm looking at one right now.... This is an ex-parrot."

Mr. Praline, Dead Parrot Sketch

"Imagine if birds were tickled by feathers. You'd see a flock of birds come by, laughing hysterically."

Steven Wright

"Courage is being SCARED TO DEATH—but saddling up anyway."

John Wayne

"That's a SECRET, private world you're looking into out there. People do a lot of things in PRIVATE they couldn't possibly explain in public ."

Det. Lt. Thomas J. Doyle, *Rear Window*

BEFORE

Cassandra sat at the drive-thru window of Taco Town, adjusting her paper hat and wishing she could move the clock forward. She was near the end of her shift, taking orders on the headset and making change, and she just wanted to get home, take off the hot uniform, and watch TV.

She worried she would get so used to saying, "Welcome to Taco Town; I'll take your order when you're ready" and "Would you like regular or huge?" that she would find those phrases cropping up in conversations away from the job.

While she was pouring her cereal one morning, her little brother had said, "Aren't you going to take my order?"

She would have smiled if it hadn't been so sad. She had become someone who handed people food. This was not what she wanted to be doing 20—or even two—years down the road. But it was a job that was close to home, and it gave her gas money. Her goal was to go to college so she wouldn't have to sit here every day breathing exhaust fumes and dealing with the endless cars and people who didn't know what they wanted.

The bell dinged, and she glanced at the monitor. A light-colored sports car. She remembered this guy from just minutes before. "Welcome to Taco Town; I'll take your order when you're ready."

He had begun to speak even before she finished. "—asked for a triple with no guacamole, and there's a ton of guacamole on here. Plus, I got a small drink, and I ordered a huge."

"I'm sorry about that, sir. If you'll pull through, we'll make sure we get that right." She said it with a smile, like her bosses instructed. Even if you were mad enough to spit, put a smile in your voice and talk slowly, and people wouldn't know you were annoyed.

This was the fourth order they'd gotten wrong today, and she couldn't help thinking there would be a fifth.

One mom had ordered three tacos with no shells. She said her kids were allergic to them, but how do you wrap a taco with no shell? They'd done the best they could. Then the lady came through again. She'd ordered a small drink, and they had given her a huge. She handed Cassandra the cup, which she had to throw away, and Cassandra had given her a small—like the woman couldn't drink what she wanted and throw away the rest.

Once a guy had pulled up and held out a vase of flowers. It might have been sweet if it had been her birthday or if she'd known the guy, but she'd told him it was store policy not to accept gifts.

The bell rang again. Finally some space between cars—things were slowing down. A man said something, but it was muffled. He tried again, but she couldn't understand. She told him to drive around.

The monitor showed an old car with big headlights. The picture was fuzzy.

His brakes squeaked as he stopped next to the window—a little too close actually.

"What can I get you—?" Cassandra gasped. Ronald Reagan. Not really Ronald Reagan—it was a wrinkled mask that looked like the old actor—the dead president. She put a hand on the counter and smiled. "You scared me there for a minute."

The masked man tilted his head, and she could tell from his eyes that something was wrong. When she saw the gun she knew she was right.

"Show me the money," the guy said. Only it wasn't his voice. It was coming from a staticky device.

She stared, too shocked to move.

"Show me the money."

Her training came back to her. She was to try to remember everything she could—how he sounded, words he used, scars, tattoos, hair. If threatened, she was to give the robber what he wanted. It was only money. And the company was insured.

She guessed there was at least $1,500 in the cash register. Maybe $2,000. Lots of 10s and 20s.

Her hands shook as she pulled a Taco Town bag from beneath the register and stuffed the money inside.

The man took it with a milky white hand. Then he tossed the bag on the passenger seat, never taking his eyes off her. Blue eyes. Deep blue.

"Don't hurt me," she said.

He sped away.

PART 1

CHAPTER 1

TUESDAY, OCTOBER 28

⊙ *Bryce* ⊙

I had just finished mowing my last lawn for the fall, which was sad. You start counting on mowing money—then you realize that the snow is right around the corner and the grass is going to turn brown and stop growing. Usually by Halloween we've had at least one snowstorm, but not this year. I wanted snow so we could get a day or two off school, but the more you want something like that, the less likely it becomes.

Ashley, my twin sister, and Dylan, my little brother, were playing pirate and damsel in distress. Dylan swatted at imaginary enemies with his plastic sword, while Ashley screamed and pushed the hair from her face like some starlet. She wants to be an actress, but she'll never admit it.

Mom watched from the kitchen, a hand over her mouth like she was trying to keep from laughing. Sam, our stepdad, wasn't home from work yet, and Leigh, our stepsister, had just gotten home from having her oil changed. Since she had gotten a car, she'd been gone a lot, mostly with her boyfriend, Randy. She poured some cereal, even though she could see that Mom was making dinner.

The phone rang, and Leigh, Ashley, and I raced for it. With three teenagers that happens a lot. Mom beat us all, but I checked the caller ID to make sure it wasn't for me. It read *Preston*.

"Oh, Jillian, I'm sorry," Mom said. "Was it sudden? . . . I'm so sorry." Mom looked a lot like she had when our dad died back in Illinois.

Mom put a hand over the phone and turned to Leigh, who punched a spoon into her soggy cornflakes. "The Prestons need to go out of town for a few days and need someone to—"

Leigh's eyes got big, and she shook her head. "No way," she whispered. "Dad's taking me to look at schools, remember?"

It sounded like she wouldn't consider helping even if she were going to be in town.

CHAPTER 2

✖ Ashley ✖

Mom took the phone to the next room, and I asked Leigh what was wrong with the Prestons' condo. "Isn't that where you stayed while the rest of us went to the Grand Canyon?"

"Right," Leigh said. "I wouldn't watch that place again for a million dollars. All those animals. All that dog food. Plus the neighbors are weird. That was the worst week of my life. And they didn't pay close to what I expected."

"A million dollars?" Bryce said.

"What's wrong with the neighbors?" I said.

"They share this courtyard, so anytime the dog goes outside he's trespassing. An old lady next door was nice but quirky. And the Preston kid—his room gave me the willies. I shut the door and went in there only to feed his snake. Gross."

. "What kind of snake?" Bryce said.

"Boa constrictor or something like that. That I had to feed it a rat turned my stomach, and the thing squealed as the snake chased it."

"Sounds cool," Bryce said.

"A family of daredevils lives in that complex too."

"Daredevils?"

"There're three of them, and they shoot each other with air pistols and ride their bikes around like they're some motorcycle gang. It was almost as bad as going on vacation with you guys."

Leigh made it sound like the Preston Prison, but I'd been there with Mom's book club, and it seemed nice.

Mom stuck her head back in. "Any ideas for someone to watch the place? It's an emergency."

Bryce said, "Ashley and I will do it."

Mom frowned.

"Yeah," I said. "We could stay there at night and walk to school. Plus there are no classes Friday."

"No way," Leigh hissed. "You guys can't handle all those . . . *creatures*!"

"You'd be surprised," Bryce said. "Mom, tell her we can come over right now, and she can show us what needs to be done."

CHAPTER 3

☺ *Bryce* ☺

"When do the Prestons leave?" I said.

"Late tonight," Mom said. "Heading for Florida."

"Did someone die?"

"Her father-in-law. Boating accident. I'd like to help, but I'm not sure I—"

"Trust me," Leigh said. "You do not want them staying there."

"You stayed there," I said.

"I'm older and have more experience."

I turned to Mom. "We can do this."

"I'm sure you can, hon, but—"

"We'll do it for free," Ashley said. "Just to help out. Besides, who else are they going to get on such short notice?"

Mom scratched her chin. "They said they don't want to impose on Mrs. Waldorf or the other neighbors. If I had more time I could ask around, but . . ."

"You're seriously thinking of letting them do it?" Leigh said.

Mom picked up the phone. "I don't know that the Prestons have a choice."

CHAPTER 4

❀ Ashley ❀

Bryce and I rode our ATVs through some pasture near our house, crossed a road, and made it to a dry creekbed that ran behind a hiking trail. From there it was only a few minutes before we pulled up to the Prestons' condo. We could see Red Rock Middle School from here.

Three large buildings—arranged in a triangle—housed two condos each. Separate from the condos was a garage with six doors.

The courtyard had the greenest grass I've seen in Red Rock. I figured they had to truck in a lot of soil and sod to get it to look so nice and then pelt it with water the whole summer. It was as green as a golf course and the ground was soft, unlike the rest of the land around town. Tall pine trees flanked the buildings, and playground equipment stood in the middle. A flower bed and nice shrubs rounded out the landscaping. It looked like a nice place to live.

Mrs. Preston had three suitcases waiting by the front door. Bryce and I kicked off our shoes and were immediately attacked by a huge dog.

"Bailey won't hurt you—unless he licks you to death," Mrs. Preston said. She had jet-black hair, was thin, and didn't wear much makeup. She always seemed to be on the move, like a hummingbird.

She handed Bryce and me copies of a printout—an animal schedule so we wouldn't get lost during the instructions. "We leave tonight for the airport, so I was hoping you'd come and let Bailey out one more time."

"Sure," Bryce said.

"You're welcome to stay here," she said. "In fact, I prefer that. Leave the patio door unlocked while you're at school, and I'll have Eulah come over and let Bailey out late morning. She'll lock up when she leaves."

"Eulah?" I said.

"Mrs. Waldorf, from next door. Sweet. A little forgetful, but you'll love her."

We followed Mrs. Preston upstairs.

"I take Bailey for a two-mile walk every morning. Of course, I won't expect you to do that, but he does need his exercise. Make sure his water and food dishes are full."

Her son's room was dark and messy, with clothes all over and . . . well, other than the posters on the walls it looked like Bryce's room, which can get a little scary.

"Binky stays in this cage," she said. "You can get him out and hold him if you like, but it's okay if you don't want to."

A five- or six-foot snake lay coiled in the corner of the cage. I appreciate God's handiwork and all, but I honestly don't understand why he had to make snakes.

"He's due for a feeding Thursday, and I left money on the front table so you can get a rat at the pet store. I would have done it myself, but—"

"No problem," Bryce said, giving me a smile. "We'll take care of it."

"Oh, and one thing that's not on the paper is Snooks." She opened the closet door, and two beady eyes stared out of the darkness. "Come on now," she cooed, picking up a white rat.

I'm more of a cat person than a rat person, but Mrs. Preston looked like she would have made a good daughter-in-law for Noah. If it crawled, slithered, or scampered, she seemed to love it.

"I bought Snooks for Binky's breakfast, but when I came back that afternoon, Binky hadn't touched him, so I figured it was meant to be. Snooks has been living in here ever since."

CHAPTER 5

◑ *Bryce* ◑

The condo was as big as a house. It had an upper level with bedrooms, a middle level with a kitchen, dining room, and living room, then a bigger area downstairs—the garden level—with a family room, another bedroom, and a utility room. It was cooler down there, and that's where the dog, Bailey, slept.

Mrs. Preston led us on a tour of three aquariums—each with different fish, food, and temperatures. We were introduced to an iguana on the South Beach Diet—at least that's what it looked like to me—and Mrs. Preston showed us the backyard and the hidden electric fence that was supposed to keep Bailey from running away but didn't really work.

Just outside the kitchen was a squawking, sharp-beaked bird the size of a 757, who could talk but wasn't in the mood. Mrs. Preston picked him up with one finger, and it looked like the bird could have crushed it with those claws. She talked like a baby to it, which always makes me sick. I guess the fact that two kids were staring at it made it nervous or something, because all the thing did was flap its wings and squawk.

"Fred will keep you company," Mrs. Preston said. "Won't you, pretty bird?"

"Pretty bird!" Fred said finally.

Mrs. Preston told us when to let Bailey out, how far to walk him, how many ounces of food he needed, and when to put him on his tether outside.

Mrs. Preston's son walked in, but she didn't even introduce him. I'd seen him at the skateboard park, where he carried his board like part of his body. He looked like a surfer without a beach—longish hair that blocked his eyes, a shirt so loose it looked like it might blow away, and jeans that had more holes than a sewer grate.

Mrs. Preston ignored him and said, "About the neighbors, Eulah—Mrs. Waldorf—is next door. She'll answer any questions." She told us about the mail and newspaper and trash and recycling. Her mind seemed to be spinning. I couldn't imagine all she was going through.

"You should probably stay away from the guy with the drums," she said. "He's not really stable." She pointed to his condo. "Just keep Bailey away from his backyard. And the kids in that unit—"

"The daredevils?" I said.

She raised a brow. "You've heard about them?"

I nodded. "I've heard about them. We'll be careful."

She opened the closet door and pointed to a huge basket. "I bought a ton of Halloween candy for Friday night. Give it out if you want. Otherwise, just leave it."

CHAPTER 6

❀ Ashley ❀

Bryce and I got home in time for leftovers.

Leigh was giving Mom and Sam an earful about everything that was going to go wrong with us watching that house. "You have to stay with those pets 24-7 or the dog will rip up the carpet. They're going to have problems."

I held up the instruction sheet. "How hard can it be?"

"Yeah," Bryce said. "We'll sleep there. It'll be like a vacation for Mom and Dylan for a couple of days."

"They're gonna mess this up," Leigh said. "Just watch. They'll kill the rabbits and—"

"Rabbits?" I said, searching the list.

"See!" Leigh screamed. "Those animals will die or they'll burn down the place and that old lady next door will choke on the smoke."

"They must have gotten rid of the rabbits," Bryce whispered.

The whole thing seemed like a test, another hoop for Bryce and me to jump through to prove to Leigh that we were worthy. She treated us like nuisances at best. Doggy doo at worst.

I wanted to throw everything in the pantry at her—including the canned goods. Leigh bugs me like no one else, and all I can do is run to my journal and write how much I hate her—well, not *her*. That wouldn't be right. But how much I hate how she *acts*, anyway.

Maybe her meanness didn't have anything to do with Bryce and me. Maybe she was mad at herself over something or was having trouble with her boyfriend. Maybe she was worried about her senior year and then having to be out on her own.

Or maybe she was just worried that Bryce and I would do a better job than she had with the Prestons' animals. Whatever it was, it made me want to kick her or pray for her. Or both.

CHAPTER 7

☺ *Bryce* ☺

At the Prestons' place that night, a note had been taped to the front door:

> Bryce and Ashley,
> I forgot to mention the rabbits. Their cages are in the downstairs bedroom. Let them out on the patio while you clean the cages, but make sure to put them back. Lots of critters would like a rabbit dinner.

Maybe Leigh was right about this whole thing.

A bark as loud as a train whistle made me cover my ears. Bailey sounded like he could have sung opera. A light from the patio silhouetted his body, the hair on his back stiffened, and his head reached my shoulders.

"It's okay, boy," Ashley said in her little-girl voice.

We walked in cautiously, but Bailey threw a fit. Ashley finally calmed him and got a leash on him. She took him out back and disappeared into the darkness.

Standing there next to the sliding-glass door gave me an eerie feeling. I was alone in the house—except for all those creatures. I heard scratching and scurrying from above, like little claws against a wall. I had to feel happy for the rat in the closet, but part of me wished the snake had been hungrier that day.

CHAPTER 8

✖ Ashley ✖

Bailey pulled me to the playground in the middle of the courtyard, tugging like a bulldozer. The dog found a metal pole, lifted his
leg, and sprung a leak that would have sunk the *Titanic*. Finally he
trotted toward some bushes at another condo.

Rap! Rap! Rap! came from inside.

Bailey stood straight, his head rising high.

Bang! Ba-bang-bang!

Drums.

Bailey snorted and his ears settled. I guessed he'd heard this
before. Through the window past the shrubs I spotted a guy inside
adjusting headphones and raising drumsticks. I wondered what the
neighbors thought of his practicing at this hour.

Bailey turned his head, and the hair on his back rose. A growl fluttered through his throat and seemed to echo through his whole body, like the rumbling of thunder. I peered into the darkness, the outline of the swing set and little slide standing between us and the other condos.

From out behind the Prestons' condo I heard footsteps and the rattle of plastic. A fox on its way from the grocery store? A bear carrying a Ziploc bag? Someone looking in windows?

Bailey tensed, but before he could bark, I grabbed his snout. "Shh."

He jerked loose and barked like a banshee—though I'm not really sure what that is. All I know is that it scared the living mustard out of me—whatever that means.

"Bailey, is that you, boy?"

Wagging his tail, Bailey bounded into the night, dragging me right through the swing set.

Bailey reared up, and I swear he was as tall as Sam. He licked the face of a wrinkled old woman, and she chuckled like she was greeting a long-lost love.

"You must be Mrs. Waldorf," I said.

"In the flesh," she said. "And you're Ashley. Jillian told me about you and your brother." She pushed Bailey away and the dog sat, sniffing at her plastic bag.

"Ma'am, do you know where Bailey's tether is?"

She pointed to a metal line that ran from one side of the condo to the other. A well-worn path in the grass showed where Bailey liked to run.

"What's in the bag?" I said.

She hesitated. "It's empty. Just like to have one with me in case."

In case what? I wondered. But I didn't ask.

CHAPTER 9

☻ *Bryce* ☻

Ashley and I locked the doors and put a wooden stick into the ridge of the sliding-glass door so it couldn't be forced open from the outside. I felt sorry for anyone trying to get past Bailey anyway.

I closed a window upstairs in Binky's room, figuring it wouldn't be good for the snake to get cold.

I didn't like this place and already regretted agreeing to stay, but there was no way I was going to admit it or slink home and let Ashley—or especially Leigh—think I was some scared little kid.

That night I had a dream that seemed to last till morning. Driving, pulsing music tore through the walls of the condo. Ashley and I

moved from the kitchen to the living room, then to an upstairs bedroom, but no matter where we went, the music stayed just as loud. I
turned on the TV to try and drown it out, but it just kept coming.
Ashley plugged her ears and cried for me to do something.

In my dream I went downstairs, thinking it wouldn't be as bad,
but it was worse. I opened the door to the rabbits' room and fell
back, gasping. The rabbits had burst from their cages and had grown
bigger than Bailey. They looked at me with red eyes and glee-filled
faces, then chased me upstairs. I yelled for Ashley to get out, but I
couldn't find her. I hoped Bailey would attack them, but he was
gone.

One of the rabbits blocked the front door, so I raced upstairs, past
pictures of the Prestons—only they weren't the Prestons anymore;
they were all big bunnies.

The bedrooms upstairs were all locked except one. I rushed inside and closed the door, leaning back against it. But Binky had
grown to the size of King Kong. More red eyes. Fangs a yard long.

I sat up in bed, sweat running down my face. This was going to be
a long house-sitting job.

PART 2

CHAPTER 10

WEDNESDAY, OCTOBER 29

Ashley

The next morning Bryce took Bailey for a walk as I started checking on the other animals. I started in Binky's room, which was the hardest for me. It wasn't that I was scared of being squeezed to death—I just didn't want to go through the whole feeding routine.

Binky stuck out his red tongue. Then I heard a voice. I thought maybe it was the answering machine. I slowly opened the door.

"Don't forget to feed the bird," came a piercing, high-pitched voice.

"Bryce? If that's you, I'm going to kill you."

"Don't forget to feed the bird." It was Fred, pacing on his perch, nodding and working his tongue. "Don't forget to feed the bird."

I put dried fruit and nuts in a bowl at the bottom of his cage, and he hopped down, picked up a piece, worked his way back to his perch, and used one claw to eat.

"Breakfast time," he squawked.

I couldn't help laughing. It might be nice to have a bird like this at our house. I said, "Guess I need to get moving, Fred." Then I went downstairs.

Bryce burst through the sliding-glass door with Bailey. "We've got big trouble," he panted.

"You forgot a plastic bag for Bailey's poop?"

"I should have taken a garbage bag. But it's not that. It's the condo across the way."

"The one with the drummer?"

"No, the one beside it. You'll never guess who lives there."

"Okay, you've got me."

Bryce braced himself like he was about to pull the pin on a hand grenade. "Principal Bookman and his wife."

"What? I didn't even know he was married. He doesn't wear a ring."

"Maybe not, but there's a woman there, and they're eating breakfast together."

CHAPTER 11

☺ *Bryce* ☺

Ashley took a long look out the patio door, but we had to keep moving. "I'll check the fish," she said, "if you'll take care of 'Bryce's bunnies.'"

"Rabbits," I said, staring her down.

She gave me an evil smile and went back upstairs.

The rabbits had eaten most of their food, so I gave them more and filled the water dishes. The smell was pungent and hard to get used to, even though the Prestons had some kind of odor-control device that made it smell less like a barn. I would never keep rabbits inside.

Seeing Mr. Bookman had scared me. I wondered if he'd heard our ATVs rumbling to the Preston place. He'd told us never to ride them to school again, but he couldn't keep us from riding them to our jobs. We'd had several run-ins with him, including a separation-of-church-and-state battle that felt like it would never end. Because of a complaint by a classmate, Lynette Jarvis, Mr. Bookman had taken down a plaque with a Bible verse on it that our friend had put up on school property. Things would probably get worse before they got better.

It's weird seeing your principal in a T-shirt and boxer shorts. The mean part of me wanted to shoot a picture of him picking his nose or something, but that wasn't right. I couldn't help wondering who the woman was. Had they secretly been married? Or was it a secret romance with a teacher?

I checked my watch. It would take us about 10 minutes to walk to school.

Ashley screamed, and I ran upstairs to find her staring at the big fish tank in the living room, the saltwater one with the most expensive fish. The biggest fish cost as much as $300 each.

Several fish floated on the surface. I tapped the side and the fish bobbed, a couple of them moving their gills slowly.

"What happened?" I said.

"Stick your hand in there and you'll see."

I put my hand in the water and jerked it out. "It's like ice." The heater in the back of the tank was off. The power cord was plugged in, but when I examined the power strip I found that the little red light was off.

My heart sank when I noticed the light switches by the door. I quickly turned on both switches, and the power came on. "When we turned the lights off last night, we turned the switch off that connects to the heater."

"Bryce, those fish are worth a lot of money."

I reached into the tank and cradled the limp body of the most colorful one. "Think we can nurse him back to health?"

She didn't think it was funny. "Why couldn't it have been the rat? I could have handled that."

"At least we know what we'll be having for dinner tonight," I said. "Bryce!"

I rummaged through the drawer below the aquarium.

"What are you looking for?" Ashley said.

"A little fish parka or sweater."

She shook her head. "This isn't funny. We *killed* them."

"It was an accident," I said. "The most we could be convicted of is fishslaughter."

That one got her. I could tell she was trying not to smile.

"Hey," I said, "if you get convicted of killing a fish, you know what they call you?"

She shook her head.

"Gill-ty."

"You are really bad."

"Think I should scale back? Get it? Huh?" I pecked on the glass. "A couple of them are still moving. Maybe they'll be okay if the water warms fast enough. But we should take the dead ones and bury them at sea."

I put them in a plastic bag, then poured them into the toilet. "Any last words?" I said.

Ashley didn't respond.

I bowed my head. "We commend these fine fish to the heavens and wish them a speedy trip to that big pond in the sky." I couldn't resist one more comment. I peeked at Ashley and said, "Well, now there are a few less things to feed."

Ashley glared at me.

CHAPTER 12

❀ Ashley ❀

When Bryce and I headed for school, we saw two kids at the playground. They yelled at each other, threw gravel, then locked in a wrestling move and rolled on the ground until someone screamed at them from a window.

"Hope they don't mess with our ATVs," I said.

An older man approached us at a good pace. Gray hair showed under his blue-and-white air force baseball cap. He had a pudgy nose and round face. "New to the neighborhood?" he said.

We told him what we were doing. He didn't seem to know who

the Prestons were, so I pointed out their condo and told him what had happened to the family.

He pursed his lips and sighed. "That's a shame. I hate to hear things like that."

"You live here?" Bryce said.

He nodded. "Been here a couple of months. Russell Harper is the name."

I introduced myself and Bryce, and he asked if we were twins. I told him I was older (by 57 seconds, but it still counts). Mr. Harper wore a wedding ring, so I asked about his wife.

His face clouded. "She passed. It'll be a year in December."

"I'm sorry."

"It's okay. It's actually nice to talk to somebody about her. We were married for 46 years."

"That's a long time," I said.

"You walk every morning?" Bryce said.

"Yeah, I try to exercise early and head for a cup of coffee at the Toot Toot Café. They make pretty good pancakes too, so I try to walk a little faster." He chuckled. "Miriam was always on me to stay in shape. She would like this place—the clean air, the mountains."

We kept walking in silence, Mr. Harper with his head down. Finally he said, "I have a hobby of raising mice. They're cute little things. If you'd ever want one or two . . ."

"We have all the pets we can stand right now," I said. "But thanks."

When we came to where we split off to go to school, Bryce told Mr. Harper to enjoy his breakfast, and he told us to have a good day. "And let me know if you need anything."

CHAPTER 13

☺ *Bryce* ☺

I'd been trying to stay away from Mr. Bookman as much as possible, but I couldn't help walking by his office and taking a look. It was all I could do not to stop and ask, "How's your girlfriend?"

In second period I was put in a group with Lynette Jarvis. She's really pretty, but she's caused a lot of trouble. Part of me wondered if her parents were the real problem, trying to make trouble for Christians.

She was in the middle of a conversation with Kael Barnes when I arrived. "I'm serious," she said. "It was in the paper today."

"What?" I said.

Lynette turned away and Kael answered, "Robbery in the Springs. Lynette says she heard some wild stuff about it."

"Like what?" I said.

Lynette suddenly warmed, probably because I was the only one interested in her story. "The paper said it was just another fast-food robbery. You know, kids looking for quick cash. But I have a friend who knows the brother of a guy who goes to school with the girl it happened to."

"Say that again," I said.

"It's reliable—that's all I'm saying. The girl's story and what's in the paper are totally different. This girl, Cassie, was almost ready to get off work at the drive-thru when a guy pulls up wearing a mask and robs her at gunpoint. I think she said it was a shotgun, and instead of talking, he plays a line from a movie. Isn't that wild?"

"What movie?" I said.

"I don't know. But isn't it interesting?"

"Yeah," I said. "It could have been a female. Or someone who doesn't want their voice recognized."

Lynette looked at me like I was her true friend. For two seconds. Then I guess she remembered I was the enemy—a Christian—and she turned back to Kael.

"How much money did the robber get?" I said.

"Thousands," Lynette said. "Or maybe hundreds, I can't remember. Cassie said the police officers said it was the same person who'd pulled some other robberies in town. They called him the Hollywood Bandit."

CHAPTER 14

❀ Ashley ❀

I couldn't help blaming myself for the fish tragedy. It was hard eating lunch because I kept seeing the poor things spinning to their final resting places. (What a way to go.)

It didn't help that Marion Quidley was eating salmon cakes. "Want to try one?" she said.

I shook my head.

"What's wrong?" Marion said. "You look sick."

"Just an upset stomach."

Hayley, my friend since moving to Red Rock, sat with us. Neither she nor Marion is a Christian, but I want them to be. It's important to have people you're praying for and trying to share the truth with. Some Christians have their spiritual hit lists and treat non-Christians like projects—they make sure they bring up God in every conversation and slip Bible verses in when they can, but Hayley and Marion are friends I want to see in heaven. I pray for them and have written about them in my journal. I share the truth any chance I get, but they're still my friends whether they believe or not.

"You guys going out Friday night?" Hayley said.

Marion licked her fingers. "I'm getting the house ready. I set up a stereo with authentic space-alien sound effects and wild-animal noises. Any kid who comes to our house will leave with his heart beating three times faster."

"How nice of you," Hayley said. "Getting into the spirit and all."

Marion crunched a celery stalk and looked at me. "I suppose you're going to be at your church dressing up as a Bible character, entertaining the kids whose parents don't believe in trick-or-treating?"

"No, I think Bryce and I are going to lie low." Bryce and I had decided we wouldn't tell anyone about our house-sitting job so no one would try to scare us with a prank.

"You're not going out?" Hayley said. "This is probably the last year I can go without looking like an idiot, so I'm going to make the most of it. We're going to get so much candy we'll be eating it for a month."

Marion said, "I think Halloween ticks off Mother Nature for some reason, because it always drops about 50 degrees that night. Rain and sleet and snow."

"Great," Hayley said. "Less competition. More candy."

Marion leaned close and lowered her voice. "I hear Boo Heckler and some of his high school cohorts are planning some weird stuff."

I had recently found out new things about Boo, the school bully. His little sister had been killed in Texas, and the whole family had been trying to deal with it. His name used to bring me shivers, but now I just felt sorry for him.

"Boo always steals candy from kids at Halloween," Hayley said. "It's like the sun coming up in the east or the pope being Catholic."

"No," Marion said. "This is not kid stuff. Remember what happened after Boo vandalized those mailboxes last spring? He says he knows who turned him in and that they're going to pay for it."

CHAPTER 15

☺ *Bryce* ☺

Ashley looked like she'd killed more expensive fish when I saw her a few minutes before last period. She grabbed my arm in a vise grip. "We need to talk."

"What's up?"

When she mentioned she'd heard something from Marion Quidley, I rolled my eyes. You have to wonder about anyone who thinks space aliens are trying to communicate with us through the backs of cereal boxes. But when Ashley explained what Marion had said about Boo, I wondered.

"What if Boo talked with someone at the police station and he knows *we're* the ones who turned him in?" Ashley whispered.

"Boo wouldn't go near the police. And no one there would tell him anyway."

"Maybe Leigh said something to Randy, and he leaked it. Not intentionally, you know. Then that got back to Boo through his evil network."

"Don't go squirrelly on me," I said. "Even if he does—"

"I'm not going squirrelly," she hissed. "This is a real threat with real consequences. You know what this guy is capable of. He backed down when you stood up to him last spring, but he wants revenge. There's no telling what might happen."

"You mean to our house?"

"To us or somebody else he thinks did this. He lost a whole summer at juvie because we turned him in."

I had just enough time to get to last period if I ran. That's when Ashley put a hand on my arm, which I hate. It means something bad is about to happen.

Boo Heckler, all six feet of him, walked past. He just stared at us like we were his mortal enemies.

CHAPTER 16

✖ Ashley ✖

On the way to the condo, Bryce and I watched for any sign of Boo. I wasn't sure which I felt worse about—Boo thinking we had turned him in to the police or his thinking it was someone else and taking it out on them.

Bailey sniffed and snorted at the door until I got it open. The patio door was locked, which meant Mrs. Waldorf had let him out.

"Tomorrow's the big day for Binky," Bryce said. "We'll have to go to the pet store and buy his dinner."

"Not me," I said. "I'm not touching that thing."

Bryce put a hand to his forehead, pretending to be sick. "I'm not feeling well," he said in a high voice. "I do hope I have the strength to make it here tomorrow."

I checked the fish tank. One was floating at the top. But Bryce was right—the others had revived.

I took Bailey for a walk, and again he had to go really bad. Our dogs, Pippin and Frodo, are tiny compared to Bailey. Their bladders have to be the size of hickory nuts. Bailey's is probably as big as a bowling ball. He stood there and stood there, balancing on three legs. This should be a dog Olympic event.

Back inside I put more food in Fred's cage, which he didn't need, and he squawked with delight. "Don't forget to feed the bird."

I opened the kitchen window to let in some air. Then we locked up and headed for our ATVs. I was strapping on my helmet when one of the daredevils slid up to us on his bike. "Those yours?"

Bryce nodded. "Yeah, and they're not toys. You and your brothers stay away from them."

He sneered. "Just asking. Good grief!" He pedaled away, and I wondered why he wasn't in school. The elementary school didn't let out for another 45 minutes.

It felt good to be back on our four-wheelers. I caught a glimpse of Mr. Bookman driving his car to his condo and held up, waiting to see which garage he was in.

"Come on, pokey," Bryce said in my headset.

The blinds in Mr. Bookman's condo were closed. I wondered about the woman in his place. Did she work during the day or stay home? Would Mr. Bookman open his door to trick-or-treaters on Halloween night or keep the lights off and pretend he wasn't there?

"What if Mrs. Preston makes us pay for the dead fish?" I said. "We'll be paying that off for years."

"She'll understand," Bryce radioed back. "It's not like we were shirking our duties."

We went home and had dinner. It was fun seeing how excited Dylan got when we rode up. You would have thought we'd been gone for a year.

Bryce's cell phone rang as we got back to the condo, and he answered. He gave me a weird look as he talked.

I went up to one of the bedrooms and waited.

CHAPTER 17

☺ *Bryce* ☺

I closed the door behind me and sat on the bed next to Ashley. She seemed even more nervous than at school. I guess because of the look I gave her.

"After what you told me," I said, "I asked Kael to keep an ear out for Boo. He rides the same bus and managed to get a seat near him. Kids around him were talking about trick-or-treating, and somebody asked Boo what his costume was."

"Boo doesn't have to dress up to be scary."

"He said he wasn't going out for candy this year, that there were other things to do. Kael asked him what he meant. Boo said there'd be some people who would never forget this Halloween."

I wasn't sure how to tell Ashley what I was about to say. She had been snooping around about Boo, trying to figure out why he was so mean, and had come across information about his past. It looked like that snooping was going to catch up with her.

She could tell I was hedging. "Tell me, Bryce."

"Boo said some people were being nosy and that he knew who ratted him out to the police. He said this Halloween is going to be payback time."

Ashley looked like she'd used tooth whitening on her face. "I did this, didn't I? His sister must have told him I was there asking questions."

"You just did it because you cared."

"I took care of those fish because I cared, and look what happened to them. Bryce, we have to do something. What if he comes over here on Halloween night?"

"Let's just be sure we're not here."

CHAPTER 18

❈ Ashley ❈

Bryce and I went for a late ATV ride back down the hill to the creekbed. The sun was setting behind the front range of mountains. In the distance, Pikes Peak showed snow on top, like a white cap on its brown head. The green pines on the hillside were interspersed with the brilliant yellow of aspens, and scrub oak leaves had turned orange. It was the most colorful time of year around here.

After we'd zoomed all over, we came back up the creek bank and slowed to avoid the grass around the condos. No sense making anyone mad by leaving tracks. As we approached the buildings, I noticed kids riding bikes through the courtyard. They were led by the three daredevils in an obvious game of follow-the-vandal, kicking up pea gravel and screaming at the top of their lungs.

Just outside his back door, Mr. Bookman looked on, hands on his hips. I hit the brakes, but Bryce didn't see him and kept going. "Don't go that way!" I radioed into Bryce's headset.

"Why? What's wrong with—?"

I could tell he had spotted Mr. Bookman. Our principal wore plaid shorts and a solid polo shirt, black socks, and dress shoes. He had chalky white legs. It would have been hard to eat after seeing that.

Mr. Bookman waved angrily and came walking toward Bryce. I told him to keep moving, but my brother just sat as if under the man's spell.

"Don't take off your helmet, and he won't know it's you," I whispered.

"He already knows," Bryce said.

I stayed way back, but I could hear the conversation over Bryce's transmitter.

"Is that you, Bruce?"

Bryce lifted his visor. "Bryce."

"I recognized you and your sister. I thought we agreed you wouldn't ride these four-wheelers anymore."

"The deal was that we wouldn't ride them to school. There's nothing wrong with us—"

"Do you know how many people are injured on these every year? And the statistics for children are worse. One reckless move and you could be killed."

Children?

"I know the dangers, sir, but we were just on our way to—"

"Do your parents know you're out joyriding?"

"Begone, you joyrider," I said into Bryce's headset.

He turned and gave me a look, then said to Mr. Bookman, "We don't drive fast, and we didn't want to hurt the grass, so we rode in the dirt."

"Well, your parents will hear from me. And if you don't stop this, I'll call the police. I can't do anything else when you're not under my jurisdiction."

CHAPTER 19

☺ *Bryce* ☺

Bailey didn't run and jump on us when Ashley opened the door. He merely stuck his head around the corner of the kitchen and whined. And the condo felt cooler. A breeze blew through that raised goose bumps on my arms.

Was someone inside?

We shut the door and stood in the darkened room. "The window," Ashley whispered. "I must have left it open this afternoon."

I thought of a bad word but didn't say it. I used to think that wouldn't happen if I became a true Christian, but it does. Not as much as it used to, but words still jump into my mind at times.

There was no screen in the window. Double bad word.

Ashley looked around the kitchen. I opened a drawer and pulled out a rolling pin. "I'll check downstairs; you check up."

"Wait," she said. "We should go together."

We tiptoed downstairs, Bailey at our heels. He slipped past us and went to the bathroom door, which was closed.

"Did you close that?" I whispered.

Ashley shrugged.

Bailey was right next to the door, sniffing and whining. He scratched with one paw the way dogs in movies do when there's a body inside an old trunk or an abandoned car.

"Stand back," I whispered. I grabbed the knob, threw the door open, yelled, and turned on the light.

Bailey looked at me like I was a madman. He sauntered inside, picked up a half-gnawed, knotted rawhide bone, and took it into the family room.

We walked back through the kitchen, turning on lights and inspecting closets. Finally we searched upstairs and came to the conclusion that no one was in the house.

Still, something was wrong, something missing. But what? The place was way too quiet.

We heard the daredevils outside, one yelling like someone was chasing him with an instrument of torture.

Ashley closed the window, locked it, and stood by the sink, deep in thought. Then she looked past me, and horror seized her face.

I turned, fearing a crazy guy with an ax was heading for me. All I saw behind me was the birdcage. The door was open.

Fred was gone.

CHAPTER 20

❋ Ashley ❋

That was why everything was so quiet. Fred had flown the coop. How long could a bird like that exist outside in Colorado? How long before some hungry cat pounced on him? Or if the daredevils saw him, they'd probably chase him with a baseball bat.

I ran out the door to the swings and found two kids I hadn't seen before. "You guys see a big bird flying around here? Or crawling or walking?"

"What color?"

"Green and . . . lots of colors."

"No."

I felt sick. First the fish and now this. I went back in and found a flashlight in the hall closet. I scanned the trees outside. Maybe Fred had perched on a balcony railing. I pointed the flashlight to the Prestons' railing, then at the condo next to us. Then I wondered how people would like someone shining a flashlight on their house. I listened for any squawking but heard only cars and dogs.

I felt a little rise in the earth and aimed the flashlight at it. Under the sod was a mound, like someone had buried something. I would have to check that out in the daylight.

A bird like Fred may have been dreaming about freedom for a long time. He could have been in Colorado Springs by now. What if he had a cousin in Florida who murdered Mr. Preston's father, knowing the family would leave Fred in the hands of teenagers like us? I was sure I was going loony.

Bryce came up beside me. "We should go back inside."

"But what if Fred gets cold? What if he gets tired and lands on I-25?"

The phone rang inside.

CHAPTER 21

◑ *Bryce* ◑

I answered just as the answering machine picked up and Mrs. Preston's voice came on. It played a short message of her and her husband alternating phrases. Fred squawked a "Hello, leave a message," and then came the beep. Ashley's face fell lower than Binky's belly when she heard the bird's voice.

"Hello, Bryce? It's Jillian Preston. How is everything going?"

"Oh, hi," I said. "Everything's okay. How are you and the family?"

"As well as can be expected. I really appreciate you two watching things, because I know you have a lot of experience. Have you bought Binky's food for tomorrow—the rat?"

"We're going to do that after school, if it's okay. You know, keep him fresh and everything."

"Yes, that's fine. Can you put me on speakerphone so I can talk to Fred? He likes it when I say good night to him."

I froze and covered the phone. "She wants to talk with Fred."

"Tell her he's asleep," Ashley whispered.

"Bryce? You still there?"

"Yes, hang on." I hit the orange button. "Okay, you're on speaker."

"Good night, pretty bird!" Mrs. Preston said. "Good night, pretty bird!" She paused. "That's funny—he usually answers. Does he look okay? Has he been eating?"

"Uh, yeah, he's been eating fine, I think." I looked at Ashley. "Getting lots of exercise. Flapping those wings like crazy."

"Good night, pretty bird," Mrs. Preston said. She sighed. "I'll call again. The funeral is Friday. We'll be home Sunday afternoon."

When I hung up, Ashley put her head on the kitchen table. "Why?" she wailed. "We've watched dogs and cats and alpacas and hamsters and even chameleons. Why does this have to happen?"

"Maybe we could buy fish that look like the dead ones," I said.

"She'll know!" Ashley howled. "You think a woman who says good night to her bird wouldn't notice that we replaced her fish? Plus those things probably cost more than our *house* is worth. This could not get any worse!"

"Sure it could. The dog could eat the snake and get hit by a car. Or we could accidentally burn the place down."

Ashley looked at me. I've seen that look only once before, the time she dropped the cordless phone in the toilet. "I'm going to bed," she said.

CHAPTER 22

❀ Ashley ❀

I pulled out my journal and wrote furiously about the feeling in the pit of my stomach when I realized the bird wasn't in his cage. I was explaining why I'd opened the window in the first place when a thought struck me: what if the daredevils had crawled into the house and taken the bird?

Bryce was watching TV when I came downstairs, some dumb old classic baseball game. I explained my theory, and he hit the Mute button. "With everything in this house, you think they'd steal the bird? Why?"

"Maybe to torture it. Let's find them." I added a whining *please* when he looked back at the TV.

"Thanks a lot! You made me miss the game winner."

I put a jacket on over my pajamas and pulled on my tennis shoes. We slipped onto the patio, keeping Bailey's black snout inside the sliding door.

A light from the parking lot lit the courtyard. The air was chilly, like summer was trying to hang on but fall was prying its fingers from the cliff, and as soon as it fell, winter would be right behind it.

"What are you doing out here?" a voice said. It was the youngest daredevil, the one with huge spaces between his teeth.

"Were you and your brothers playing at the Preston house today?" I said.

He scrunched up his face. "What would we be doing over there? They don't let us have any fun." He looked at my shoes and pajama bottoms. "You go to bed this early?"

Bryce stepped in. "We're looking for their bird. Tell us where it is, and we won't tell anyone you took it."

"I don't know nothin' 'bout no bird," he said, his face as full of wrinkles as a 90-year-old man's. He looked past us, craning his neck. "*There's* somebody who might know. Weirdest person in the neighborhood. You know what she does out here at night?"

Mrs. Waldorf came out on her back porch, carrying something.

"She's out here at all hours," he said. "Heard she used to live in some crazy house. Cut people up or something. You know anything about her?"

This kid was one walking question mark. I had the feeling he was asking what time dinner was served as soon as he was born. Bryce and I shook our heads, staring at Mrs. Waldorf.

"What *would* she be doing out here at this time?" I said.

"Taking her cat for a stroll?" Bryce said.

The kid headed for his house. "You two go ahead and get killed. I'm going inside."

Bryce and I scooted back toward some shrubs by the Preston house. Mrs. Waldorf carefully placed a plastic bag on a small table, picked up a garden spade, and strolled into the courtyard. She punched a hole in the sod and pulled a layer back, then went to work on the ground underneath.

"Is she putting in a new sprinkler system?" I said.

"Looks like she's planting something, but they have a gardener."

She carefully shoveled the dirt to the side of her deck until the hole was big enough. Then she took the plastic bag and gingerly put it in. After she studied her work, she covered the hole with dirt and put the sod back in place, mashing down the edges.

"I think she's done this before," Bryce said.

PART 3

CHAPTER 23

THURSDAY, OCTOBER 30

◎ *Bryce* ◎

I had a plan for how to handle Boo Heckler. Ashley and I would tell him that Jeff Alexander had given his name to the police last spring. We'd tell him Jeff had been the reason Boo went to the juvenile detention center.

Jeff had died in the meantime, so Boo couldn't hurt him and it would take the heat off Ashley and me. It almost felt like Jeff would be helping us one more time.

The problem was, it was a lie. Plus, it felt like we would be disrespecting Jeff's memory, and Boo would probably see right through it.

Ashley and I agreed we couldn't tell Boo the truth that it was us, but we also couldn't let someone else pay the penalty, even Jeff.

I composed a note in my head, and Ashley dug out an envelope addressed to the school from a trash can in the office. We figured that would throw Boo off. We couldn't let Ashley write it because she has classes with Boo, and he would recognize her handwriting, which looks like one of those fancy signatures on the Declaration of Independence. Mine looks like a chicken's with bad eyesight. Using red ink, I wrote in my usual jagged scrawl.

> Aaron,
>   I know you want to pay back the person who turned you in to the police and that you have something planned for Halloween night. You're making a big mistake.
>   If you hurt the wrong person, you'll hurt only yourself, because I will tell the police. I might even videotape you to prove it.
>   Watch out.
>   Be careful.
>   The prank you pull may come back to you.
>   Signed,
>   A friend

"That'll freak him out," Ashley said.

Just before the bell rang for next period, Ashley and I dropped the letter into Boo's locker.

CHAPTER 24

❦ Ashley ❦

I couldn't eat. I kept thinking of the dead fish, the open window, and the look sure to be on Mrs. Preston's face when she discovered her "pretty bird" was gone. Someone offered me a cookie at lunch, but all I could see was the rat Bryce and I had to buy at the pet store after school, and I pushed it away.

My last class was right outside Boo's locker, so I watched as he walked down the hall, arms swinging like an ape's. He was trying to grow a mustache and beard, but it wasn't working. It looked more like the fuzz you see on peaches, and even that hadn't come in well.

When he opened his locker, the letter fell out. He put some books inside, grabbed an apple, and ate like a cow, chewing from right to left, then ignored a huge trash can in the corner and put the core back in his locker and closed the door.

He was about to leave when he saw the letter. He opened it, and I watched his lips move. He looked around to see if he was being watched—or videotaped?—so I ducked inside my classroom.

The pet store was packed with cages, pet food, aquariums, and supplies. A row of puppies whined and barked, scratching at the glass. One lay on its back, yawning and playing with shredded newspaper.

It was all I could do to get to the counter with Bryce, squeezing through the massive stacks of birdcages and racks of dog leashes. Bryce tapped me on the shoulder and pointed at a perch in the corner. There sat a bird that looked like Fred. I wanted to ask the owner if the thing had flown in during the past couple of days. The sign underneath said $500.

Bryce started to explain the type of snake we needed to feed, but the store owner stopped him. "You mean Mrs. Preston's snake? Binky?" The man was tall and fleshy and had a tattoo of some animal on one arm chasing another animal on the other.

"Jillian said you'd be in," the man said, grabbing white cardboard and folding it into a box. It had a yellow smiley face on each side. "Binky likes the large white ones."

"Yummy," Bryce said.

The rats were kept in a cage within sight of the snakes, which I thought was cruel. The snakes could keep an eye on their lunches, kind of like people do at Subway.

"Here we go," the owner said, picking up a rat by the tail and dropping him into the box. He secured the top with tape. The little animal scratched and scurried in the box.

Bryce looked at me. "I'll pay and you carry him home."

Not a chance.

As we neared the condo, two daredevils rode past, whooping and hollering like little cavemen back from their bison hunt. When we got to the door, Bryce held out a hand.

"What?"

"The key."

"I thought you had it," I said. "You locked the door this morning."

He gave me the same look I had given him when he suggested I carry the rat. "Ash, that's not funny. Let me have it."

I tried the door. Locked. "I'm serious. I don't have it."

"You opened the door last night," he said, going through his pockets. "What did you do with the key?"

I searched my backpack, my pockets, even my socks. "I must have put it on the table when I saw the window was open."

Bryce put the box down and ran around back. He returned with a glum look. "Everything's locked."

CHAPTER 25

☺ *Bryce* ☺

I yelled at Ashley. I called her stupid. I checked all the windows, the sliding patio door, even in the flowerpot. Nothing.

Bailey barked and scratched like a dog who really needed to get to his favorite tree or fire hydrant. I stared at my sister, and she sobbed. That made me feel bad, and I apologized for yelling at her and calling her stupid.

"We'll get you out of there in just a minute, Bailey," she cooed.

I knocked on Mrs. Waldorf's door, and when she opened it, her cat ran out. "Oh, it's all right. He'll be back."

"Do you have a spare key for the Prestons'?" I said.

"Sure do," she said. Wonderful Mrs. Waldorf. Strikingly beautiful in her old age. She invited us in. "Now let me think." She scratched her head. "I told myself I'd put it where I wouldn't forget."

"Maybe on your key ring," Ashley tried.

"I don't think so. . . ." She pulled her key ring from her purse. There were a bunch of keys on it. "No," she said, "it had a piece of tape with their name on it."

"Maybe she buried it in the backyard," I whispered.

"Oh, I remember," she said, chuckling. She opened the front closet, and there was a rack with a garage-door opener and several keys.

"I don't see one for the Prestons'," I said.

"No, that's right. They borrowed mine to give to you."

I groaned and Ashley slumped into a chair. The dominoes of our lives were knocking each other over in a long line, and it didn't look like it would end soon.

I asked to see Mrs. Waldorf's phone book. "We have to get a locksmith out here before Bailey floods the place. Either that or break a window, and the lock's probably going to cost less."

I found a locksmith's number, and while I was talking I noticed a bunch of plastic bags in the corner, much like the one we had seen Mrs. Waldorf with the night before. On the table was a candle circled with blurry photos.

When the man told me how much it would cost to unlock the door, I knew I had to go home and scrounge up the cash. "Stay here and wait for the guy," I told Ashley.

I rushed to my ATV but stopped in my tracks when I heard Bailey going berserk inside the house. He barked and slobbered all over the front window. On the windowsill was Mrs. Waldorf's cat, licking a paw and looking satisfied.

On the ground was the white box from the pet store. It was torn open. And empty. The cat had just eaten his happy meal.

CHAPTER 26

❦ Ashley ❦

The locksmith showed up in a yellow truck with big blue lettering. He wore a belt that held a bunch of tools.

Mrs. Waldorf had taken her cat inside. I didn't tell her he had stolen Binky's dinner, but I knew we'd have to get back to the pet store before it closed. This was getting to be one expensive day.

It took me a while to convince the locksmith that I was actually in charge of the house. When he saw Bailey pawing at the front door and Mrs. Waldorf confirmed our problem, he went to work.

"Wait, how are you going to pay for this?" the man said.

"My brother went home to get our money. He should be back soon."

It took the locksmith less than five minutes to get the door open. Bailey had left a wet spot on the carpet. I unlocked the patio door, and he loped out the back.

I grabbed the key from the kitchen table and slung it around my neck. I wasn't going to lose it again. I'd sleep with it if I had to.

The locksmith cleared his throat and handed me a pink sheet. "How did you want to pay?"

I froze when I saw the $125 total. "Uh, my brother will be right back."

"You said that a while ago." He stomped off, taking his tools to his truck. I was glad when I heard Bryce's ATV.

Bryce handed the man a wad of cash. "I had $35, Ash. You had $27, and Mom had left $30 on top of the refrigerator for Leigh."

"You stole it?"

"I borrowed it. It was an emergency. What was I supposed to do?"

"You're short $33," the man said.

"We can pay you as soon as the owners get back," I said. "They're going to—".

"I need payment in full at the time of service," he said.

Bryce snapped his fingers. "Wait right here," he said, running inside and coming back with the phone book. He pulled out a coupon. "I saw this when I looked you up. I save 25 percent off our first job." Bryce punched numbers into his watch calculator. "We still owe you $1.75."

The man shook his head. "Call it even, kid. Hope the owners make it up to you when they get back."

The rat, the stain on the carpet, the aquarium, the bird . . .

We'll be lucky to break even.

CHAPTER 27

☺ *Bryce* ☺

While Ashley cleaned the carpet, I ran back to the pet store, only to find the door locked and the neon Open sign turned off. I raced back and helped Ashley feed the rest of the animals.

She showed me a stain on the stairs that looked like bird poop, and we figured it was just Fred getting excited about his freedom before he flew through the window.

As we ate dinner, all I could think about was how we were going to feed Binky. If I could just make him a peanut-butter sandwich or throw him a hot dog, it could see him through another day, but I had a sick feeling there was only one thing we could do. No way was I going to let that snake die.

Ashley shrieked, "Come look at this!"

The TV news showed a reporter standing outside Burger Barn in Red Rock. Ashley turned up the volume.

". . . robbery here in this small town, which fits the same description as several in Colorado Springs the past few weeks. The gunman reportedly pulled up to the window, played a movie clip that demanded money, then sped away."

The camera pulled back, showing two teenagers.

"That's Randy!" Ashley shouted.

Randy is Leigh's boyfriend, who plays just about every sport under the sun—though baseball and football are his best. His hair stuck out from under his baseball cap, and he stood beside the reporter, grinning like he had just won the lottery.

"The workers at the restaurant are still being questioned by police, but we have an eyewitness to the robbery. Randall Frazier, tell us what happened."

Randy smiled, and his gaze darted toward the camera. "Well, we just came over after football practice and were having some burgers and shakes when this car pulls up. When you're in the dining room you can hear people on the speaker ordering stuff. It was weird. Somebody played a clip from a movie I'd seen a long time ago. I recognized the voice.

"There was a commotion, because I think somebody fainted, and then the car pulled away. I didn't get the license-plate number or anything."

Someone punched Randy's arm and gave him a high five. I wondered what Leigh would say when she found out her boyfriend was a TV star.

Another mystery in Red Rock, and in the midst of feeding all these animals, Ashley and I were going to try to solve it.

CHAPTER 28

❋ Ashley ❋

For fun Bryce and I hopped on our ATVs and drove by Randy's place. We found him outside with a bunch of his friends. They were talking and laughing about the big interview.

Bryce and I asked if Randy had seen more than he had said during the interview. "Do you remember anything about the car?" I said.

"Yeah, it was a light color, white or cream or something like that, with a white top. An old car like they have at car shows."

"So it was from the '30s?" Bryce said.

"Nah, '50s, maybe early '60s. In great shape as far as I could tell. Got up to speed pretty fast."

"Which way did it go from the Burger Barn?" Bryce said.

"Toward the interstate. Then there was so much shouting from the back room that I lost sight of it. They were also trying to help the girl at the window. The one who collapsed."

Randy explained the movie clip one more time, and I wrote down the words. He also said he heard the guy wore a Frankenstein mask, but he didn't see it.

As Bryce and I rode back toward town we could see the Burger Barn across the interstate. Police cars were still parked outside.

"You think the thief could be living right here in Red Rock?" I asked Bryce through the headset.

Bryce shrugged as he motored into the creekbed and up the embankment.

Mr. Bookman and his wife or lady friend stood on his balcony watching us.

CHAPTER 29

☺ *Bryce* ☺

Ashley and I were so busy with the animals that it became harder and harder to think of solving a robbery. Besides, whoever had done it probably lived far away.

Ashley and I made sure Bailey had enough water in his dish and was let out one more time. I joined Ashley upstairs in Binky's room and opened the closet door.

"What are you doing?" she said.

"Binky's about to eat his cage. We have to take drastic action."

"You're not thinking of—?"

"It's our only option if he wants to eat tonight."

"Bryce, Mrs. Preston loves Snooks. You can't make him snake food."

"What if we just put him in there like she did and see what happens? If Binky eats him, we get another rat. If he doesn't, we feed him a different one tomorrow."

"Mrs. Preston will *know*. She probably has Snooks's birthmarks memorized."

"Got a better idea?"

Binky eyed us and stuck out his tongue. I wondered how long it would take a snake to starve.

I moved some clothes and found Snooks in a little shoe box on top of an old guitar amplifier. I grabbed him by the tail. Snooks twitched his nose and sniffed. He probably thought he was going to be petted and fed rather than made to walk the plank.

I held him over Binky's cage, but Ashley told me to stop. "Let me look on the Internet and see what it says," she said.

I looked the rat in the eyes. "You just got a last-minute reprieve from the governor."

CHAPTER 30

✖ Ashley ✖

I found a lot about feeding snakes online. One sign that your snake is hungry is increased activity, which fit Binky. It also said you should keep a snake on a regular feeding schedule. There was information on the size of mouse or rat to feed your snake and how different snakes eat, and I saw really gross pictures, but nothing said how often to feed one.

"Maybe we should just call Mrs. Preston," I said. "I'm tired of keeping all this from her."

"You want to tell her about Fred?"

"No, that can wait."

"Go ahead," Bryce said.

"No, we'll flip for it."

Bryce tossed a coin, and I yelled heads before it hit the carpet.

George Washington's profile was the best thing I'd seen all day.

CHAPTER 31

☺ *Bryce* ☺

My heart banged against my rib cage as the line rang in Florida. I tried to get my mind off what I was about to do. I looked out the sliding-glass door and saw Mr. Harper's condo. Light from a television flickered in the window. Mr. Bookman's condo was lit up like daytime inside. The three daredevils were crouching behind the playground equipment and shooting BB guns at each other. They wore protective goggles, but I just knew someone was going to rush inside crying soon. The sound of drums came from another condo.

When someone picked up, I slammed the phone down.

"What?" Ashley said.

"I don't want to bother them."

"You lost—you have to ask her. What if that snake dies? Mrs. Preston said he's something like 30 years old. She's had him longer than she's been married."

"What about Mr. Harper? He raises mice, right?"

"Too small."

"Maybe two then. Something to tide Binky over. A snake snack." That made her smile.

"Come on, Ash. Let's give it a try."

CHAPTER 32

✖ Ashley ✖

Mr. Harper's condo was like the others, except the front faced the garage across the street and didn't have decorations or lawn ornaments like Mrs. Waldorf's. She had bird feeders and even a pink flamingo.

Bryce was about to knock when the door opened and Mr. Harper appeared with a couple bags of trash. "Hello there," he said cheerily.

"Need some help?" I said, taking one of the bags.

"Neighborly of you!"

From the smell I could tell Mr. Harper liked bananas.

"Just put it down right there," he said. "I'll get the recycle stuff later."

"You sure?" Bryce said. "Glad to help."

"Well, that would be wonderful. I usually make two trips for all the papers, but I'll bet you could carry them all at once."

His house looked like a shrine to old movies. He had posters of everyone from Humphrey Bogart to Jimmy Stewart to Judy Garland. The TV station he had on showed a black-and-white movie in between commercials for motorized wheelchairs and life insurance.

His bookshelves contained lots of photography books about famous films like *Gone With the Wind, The Godfather,* and *The Wizard of Oz.* He even had shooting scripts for several movies. I leafed through his script for *Citizen Kane.*

"Now there's a movie," he said. "I like to watch a film and follow the script to see what was added or deleted."

"You must like movies a lot," I said.

Mr. Harper chuckled. "One of the fun memories of my youth was going to the picture show every Saturday. It cost only pennies back then. And the movies were a lot better. I met my wife in a movie theater."

"Was it love at first popcorn?" Bryce said.

Mr. Harper laughed again. "It was for me. It took Miriam a little longer to realize we were made for each other. You see, I was 10 and she was 12. It took me eight years to get her to go out with me, and our first date—"

"Was to the movies," I said.

"Actually we went bowling—a terrible idea because I don't bowl. But that's the only place she'd agree to go. The second date we saw Burt Lancaster—she used to think I looked like him. I always thought she looked like Ingrid Bergman."

I have no idea who these people are. But can I ask for a mouse to keep a snake alive without listening to a few stories?

"Have you ever seen *Driving Miss Daisy*?" Mr. Harper said, pulling a DVD off his shelf. "It's one of the last movies Miriam and I watched before she passed. You can borrow it if you like."

I had seen it, but I took it anyway.

"Movies, like books, can enrich your life," Mr. Harper said. "Or they can do the opposite. All depends on what you see."

CHAPTER 33

☺ *Bryce* ☺

I carried out the heavy green newspaper bin while Ashley made small talk with Mr. Harper. I figured she'd have a mouse or two by the time I finished with the other bins, but when I returned she didn't even seem close to asking.

Mr. Harper had launched into a story about a movie called *Birdman of Alcatraz,* and I figured that was a good time for me to ask for one of his mice.

"Animal lovers, are you?"

"We have two dogs at home, some fish—Ashley has a cat too."

"Patches," Ashley said.

He told us about his mouse collection and their breeding habits and a bunch of other stuff that would have been interesting if we didn't have a famished snake on our hands. Finally he asked us to wait in the living room while he went upstairs.

"Movies and mice," Ashley said. "Perfect combo."

"At least it keeps him busy," I said.

"He seems lonely. Wonder if he's ever met Mrs. Waldorf."

"If he has, she probably doesn't remember it."

"That's not very nice."

Mr. Harper came back with a little box—the kind they serve Chinese food in, and I thought that was appropriate since this little fellow was going to be Binky's dinner.

"Do you have somewhere you can keep him?" Mr. Harper said.

"Oh, we have just the place," I said.

Ashley kicked me.

"I name all my little friends after characters in the movies. His name is Ishmael, from *Moby Dick*." He opened the box, and the white mouse looked up with pleading eyes.

"Ah," Ashley said. "So cute."

"I hope you enjoy him. And if you ever need any more, you know where to come."

We thanked him and made our way to the Preston condo. "Should have named this little guy Ahab."

"Why's that?" Ashley said.

"Isn't he the captain who gets eaten by Moby Dick?"

CHAPTER 34

✖ Ashley ✖

Bryce made me go with him to lift the top of Binky's cage, but he couldn't make me watch. I held the carton as Bryce grabbed the poor mouse by the tail. The little guy seemed to know something was up. Binky pressed against his glass enclosure like he was at a slither-thru ordering Mice McNuggets.

"Any last words?" Bryce said.

"Just do it."

"Maybe we should say grace."

"Bryce!"

"For what he is about to receive, may he be truly thankful. . . ."

The mouse plopped to the bottom of the cage. "We have touch-down. Binky's going for the takedown."

"Bryce! I don't want a play-by-play."

I stomped off and tossed the box in the trash.

When Bryce said, "Binky's opening his jaws, and Ishmael is on his final voyage," I hurried downstairs. I wished we'd listened to Leigh and not taken this job. Life was complicated enough with Boo Heckler and our schoolwork.

Mr. Harper's house was dark except for light flickering against the back wall. He sat in his tattered easy chair eating something. Looked like popcorn.

Mrs. Waldorf was on her patio gazing at the stars as her cat made its way around the backyard. He must have been full of Binky's original rat.

I glanced back at Mr. Harper's condo, and something clicked. Old movies. The Burger Barn robbery. The thief always wore a mask and drove an old car and played movie dialogue through the car speakers.

Nah! Mr. Harper was a sweet old man. Wouldn't harm a fly. I couldn't imagine him *ever* doing something like that.

Bryce came downstairs slowly and looked out the window.

"What's wrong?" I said.

"I was just thinking about the robbery. What if Mr. Harper . . . ?"

"I was thinking the same thing. But he doesn't seem the type, does he?"

"One way to find out."

CHAPTER 35

☺ *Bryce* ☺

I snatched the garage-door opener from the closet and a
flashlight a little low on batteries. I figured Ashley and I would be
able to get in Mr. Harper's garage and see if there was an old car. It
was a long shot, but if we found such a car, we could call the police.
Case closed.

But when the garage door creeped up on both Preston stalls, I realized each of these was walled off from the others. Instead of one
huge garage, there were six individual garages with two spaces
each. Mr. Preston's car was there—a hybrid gas/electric plugged

into an outlet in the back—along with some oil, antifreeze, and jumper cables on a small metal shelving unit in the corner.

We closed the door and were headed back to the Prestons' house when the next garage door opened.

Ashley and I ducked behind the end of the Prestons' garage and watched a short man with bushy hair walk toward us. He wore loose, dark clothing and carried a bag. Only one car was in his garage—a boxy, European thing. This had to be the drummer. He was the only one we hadn't met, and anyway drumsticks stuck out of his bag.

I stepped out and said hello.

The man froze. "Who are you?"

"My sister and I are watching the Preston place while they're away."

"So you're taking care of the farm?" he said, smirking. "Good luck."

"We heard somebody around here has a really old car. Something from the '50s or '60s. Ever seen anything like that?"

He paused. "Not that I remember."

On our way back to the house we heard rustling and whispers across the courtyard. Ashley and I tiptoed between buildings. The two older daredevils crouched by the sidewalk, placing something there and covering it. We waited until they made it around the corner and went to inspect.

At each crack in the sidewalk we found a piece of duct tape hiding an M-80, a high-powered firecracker.

"What are they up to?" Ashley said.

"Probably planning to scare some trick-or-treaters tomorrow night."

CHAPTER 36

❀ Ashley ❀

Bryce and I stayed inside with the lights off, watching the kids plant their surprises. We planned to pull out the fuses early the next morning if we could get up before they did.

"Think we'd find any clues in Mr. Harper's trash?" I said.

"Like what?"

"Maybe a Burger Barn bag." I pursed my lips. "I really want to make sure he's not involved. He seems like such a nice old man."

Just before midnight we crept back outside. The temperature had dropped, and the wind moved tree branches. Bottles and paper from recycle bins skittered along the street, making weird noises.

"Something's blowing in over the mountain," Bryce said, pointing to the range that runs by Red Rock from Colorado Springs to Denver. "If that happens, those M-80s will be soaked."

Marion Quidley had said Mother Nature hated Halloween.

When we got to Mr. Harper's garbage, Bryce scowled. "Didn't we help him carry two bags out here? There are three now."

The third was smaller and sat atop the other two.

"Is it illegal to go through people's trash?" I said.

Bryce shrugged. "Trash is trash. Once you put it out here, it's abandoned."

The bag was double tied and took a few moments to open. I wanted to tear it, but Bryce said we shouldn't. We finally got it open but couldn't see anything because it was so dark. It certainly wasn't as stinky as the other bags.

Bryce turned on his flashlight, but just as he was about to shine it inside, a light came on behind us. We scurried into the darkness. The light finally went off, but neither of us felt safe enough to go back to the garbage.

"Did you see anything in there?" I whispered.

"Not sure, but I thought I saw rubber at the top, like a mask."

"Let's check it out," I said.

Bryce shook his head and pointed to an upstairs window. A cigarette glowed. "Mr. Harper is watching."

PART 4

CHAPTER 37

☺ *Bryce* ☺

Ashley stayed in the main bedroom upstairs, but I camped out on the couch in the living room. Normally with no school the next day, I would have found some late-night game on TV, but I couldn't tear myself away from the window at the back of the house. I watched Mr. Harper's place, but the lights remained off.

Most interesting was Mr. Bookman's condo. Just after midnight the lights were still on, and the woman sat at the kitchen table. The window must have been open because I heard her phone every time it rang, and it must have rung 50 times before I went to sleep. She'd pick it up, type on her laptop, then hang up and wait for another call.

What in the world was she doing? Why would anyone stay up all night answering the phone?

Ashley woke me getting some cereal in the morning. I ran to the window. The woman was gone from Mr. Bookman's kitchen, and all the lights were out.

"Sleep well?" I said.

"I've been on roller coasters where I got more sleep. I dreamed that bird talked to me."

"Surprised you didn't dream about Ishmael."

"Thanks for reminding me when I'm trying to eat."

"What are brothers for?"

"How'd *you* sleep?"

"Same as you, but no dreams." I told her what I'd seen at the Bookman place.

"Weird," she said. "And he wasn't there?"

I shook my head.

She put her spoon down. "I don't know if it's a good idea to spy on people. Would we like people watching our family every day?"

Ashley's words stung. If you try to live by the Golden Rule, "Do unto others as you would have others do unto you," then you probably wouldn't secretly watch them. I wouldn't want Boo Heckler out there with binoculars. But we were detectives—snooping in trash, opening garage doors.

There was a screech of air brakes and a green Waste Management truck pulled in front of Mr. Harper's condo.

"We forgot to put the trash out," I said.

CHAPTER 38

✖ Ashley ✖

Bryce and I scrambled to the pantry and grabbed the trash bags. We burst outside as the truck flew past.

"This is turning out to be a really awful week," I said. "Besides everything else, the Prestons' house will smell like garbage."

"It already smells like animals," Bryce said. "Let's put this in the garage, where we won't have to smell it."

The clouds over the mountains had given way to a thick, white fog that loomed over the town like a mile-wide ghost. The wind had died, but it was cooler, like we were in for something more than clouds.

We stacked the trash bags in the back of the garage and came out to the three daredevils.

"Nice pj's," the oldest said. He wore a black Raiders hat, a sure sign of rebellion in Bronco territory. He looked like he wanted to be hurt.

"You guys going trick-or-treating in those outfits?" another said.

All three laughed, but the youngest laughed the loudest and longest.

I could tell by Bryce's red face that he was through being nice. Usually kids this age treated eighth graders with some respect. These kids obviously didn't care how much older we were.

"You guys know M-80s aren't allowed in town," Bryce said. "They could really hurt little kids walking by."

Raider Hat scowled. "Who said we were going to shoot off M-80s?" He looked offended that we would even bring up the subject.

"Yeah, who said that?" the little one said.

"If any of those go off tonight, we'll tell the police who did it," Bryce said.

CHAPTER 39

☺ *Bryce* ☺

Binky moved like he was still hungry, so I headed to the pet store. On my way to the ATV, Mr. Harper walked by. His face lit up. "Bryce, thanks again for helping with the trash last night. How's Ishmael?"

"Oh, I really couldn't say."

"Well, let me know if you need any food for him."

The pet-store owner stifled a smile when he heard what had happened to our first rat. "You sure you didn't eat it yourself and have to come back for seconds? Tell you what, I'll give you 50 percent off the second one. Just don't tell Mrs. Preston I did that."

I went by the Toot Toot Café and noticed Mr. Harper laughing with Mr. Crumpus, the owner. Mr. Harper was in the no-smoking section, which I thought a little odd.

When I neared the condos I heard someone scream. It sounded scary because it was coming from Sheep Horn Hill, one of the steepest, most treacherous dirt roads in Red Rock. The hill circled up a steep slope near Kangaroo Rock, and at the top cell-phone towers had been made to look like pine trees. Twice a year the road was graded and smoothed, but most of the time it was full of ruts and holes. No one with a car they cared about drove that way. The hill was also dangerous for kids on bikes, because if you went too fast there wasn't any way to stop except to drive off the road into barbed wire. Gravel and chunks of dirt could throw even a good rider.

"Help!" someone yelled and waved. I recognized the black-and-silver hat. The Raider daredevil. "My little brother crashed!"

CHAPTER 40

✖ Ashley ✖

Bryce ran inside and told me what had happened. He put a white box on the kitchen table. "Get to your ATV."

We zoomed toward Sheep Horn Hill, talking to each other through our headsets. "Why didn't you call 911?" I said. "Or check with their parents?"

"I knocked on their door. No answer. I'm not sure if this is real or not. Could be a trap. I want to make sure before we get anyone else involved."

We slowed as we came to the bottom of the hill. This was a remote area where lots of motorcycle and BMX bikers hung out, so we didn't want to go flying up the hill and hit one of them.

Bryce and I parked, took off our helmets, and started up the hill. As soon as we rounded the first bend, I heard someone whimper. The road doubled back in what looked like the end of the sheep's horn, the steep bank taller than our heads and tree roots reaching out like gray fingers. The farther we walked, the darker it got, though it was daylight.

When we turned the corner, I noticed several places where cars had spun into the embankment. Any kid riding down this road full tilt could reach such a terrific speed there was no way they could make the corner. In fact, I'd heard of one kid who'd gone airborne over the bank and landed in the branches above us.

At the top of the hill we spotted a group bending over someone. The middle daredevil's bike lay 20 yards away, the front rim bent at an ugly angle. The rider lay tangled in barbed wire. None of the three was wearing a helmet. When I saw the kid's right leg, I gasped. Blood covered his ankle and shoe. His arms and hands were scraped, and a bruise already colored his chin. Tears ran down his dirty cheek.

Another person had joined the daredevils. He was bigger, with long, gangly arms. He stood when he saw us coming.

Boo Heckler.

CHAPTER 41

☺ *Bryce* ☺

Had Boo put the daredevils up to something, trying to trap Ashley and me? He'd wanted to ride our ATVs for months, had even threatened us about it. I looked back down the hill, wondering whether someone might be trying to steal them.

But this was no trap. If this kid was faking an injury, he deserved an Academy Award.

"His leg's caught in that wire," Boo drawled, "and every time he moves, it goes deeper."

"How did you find them?"

"I was working on my car and heard screaming." Boo had tools in his pants pocket.

"You have pliers?" I said.

Boo pulled out a wrench, two screwdrivers, and red-handled pliers. They had wire cutters.

"Help me!" the kid said through clenched teeth. "I don't want to bleed to death."

One of the barbs—the sharp stickers in the wire—had embedded itself in the kid's skinny leg.

"I don't think the wire hit an artery or anything," I said, trying to calm him. "You're gonna be okay." I looked at Boo. "Think you can cut through that wire?"

"You don't want to take it out?"

"No, we should cut it on both sides and get him to a doctor."

"Mom will kill us if we take him to a doctor," Raider Hat said.

"It could get infected," Ashley said.

The hurt kid yelped, and I figured it was time to do what we had to do. I showed Boo where to cut.

"Farmer's gonna be ticked off that I ruined his fence."

"He'll get over it," I said.

Boo grunted and strained. His face turned red, and I thought his veins were going to pop out of his neck. The wire finally snapped and the kid screamed.

Boo started on the other side, gritting his teeth, sweating, mashing the pliers together. I never would have been able to do what he did.

When the wire snapped the second time, the kid collapsed and writhed on the ground. He'd ripped a hole in his pants, and his elbows were badly skinned.

"What do we do now?" Raider Hat said. "We don't want no doctor or hospital or anything."

"My ma used to be a nurse," Boo said. "She's home." He looked at me. "Can you help me carry him?"

"I have a better idea," I said.

CHAPTER 42

❀ Ashley ❀

Bryce drove his ATV slowly up the hill and was working with Boo to try to get the injured kid aboard when a cloud of dust rose and a rumbling grew louder.

"Motorcycles!" I yelled.

We hopped up on the bank as five dirt bikes roared past, kicking up dirt and rocks, barely missing Bryce's ATV. He gave me a look like I had saved their lives.

I was glad Boo had happened on the scene. It would have taken us a lot longer to get the kid—who we learned was named Tyler—

free. Still, Boo worried me. Did he know Bryce and I were responsible for his being sent to juvie? Had someone told Boo we were the ones who put the note in his locker?

The other two daredevils rode their bikes behind Bryce, and I followed on foot. They kept trying to get him to go faster, but Bryce wouldn't listen. He asked Boo a question, then got on his cell phone as they started down a steep hill.

Boo's little sister ran outside in a princess costume, and her mother followed. After inspecting Tyler's leg, she said, "We need to get him inside."

Boo grabbed Tyler and carried him inside on his back. When I reached Bryce's ATV, I saw blood on the seat and down the side. I found a garden hose and washed it off.

When Bryce and Boo came out, Bryce said, "I need to find that farmer and tell him about the fence."

"He lives back there," Boo said, pointing. "I can take you."

I went in to check on Tyler and to offer to go back to the condos with the other two daredevils. I caught Bryce's arm and whispered, "Be careful."

CHAPTER 43

☺ *Bryce* ☺

Boo led me up the hill behind his house through a grove of pine trees as thick as any I'd seen in Colorado. He walked so fast that I was sure he'd walked this way lots of times.

I finally caught up to him. "Thanks for helping with the kid," I said.

"Yeah. Didn't know he was a friend of yours."

I explained that he was just a neighbor of the people whose house we were watching.

"Where?"

I told him before remembering that Ashley and I had agreed we were going to keep that to ourselves.

"What are you doing tonight?" I said.

Boo shrugged. "Why?"

I think things happen for a reason—like running into Boo away from school—so I decided to be bold. A few months ago I'd been so scared of Boo that the thought of him made me sweat or lose sleep.

"Somebody told me you were up to something tonight," I said. "Said it might be spectacular."

He stopped and leaned against a tree. "Who?"

"Who?"

"I'm not imitating an owl."

I laughed like it was the best joke in the history of comedy, but I was really trying to think of what to say. A guy who can clip barbed wire has to be treated with respect.

"Good one," I said. "But it's not really important who said—"

"It is to me," Boo said. "I got a warning that somebody's watching me. Threatening me. I don't like that."

"I don't blame you. I wouldn't either."

"So who told you this about tonight?"

I scrambled farther up the hill. "Let's just say I heard you're trying to get someone back for sending you to juvenile detention last summer."

Boo followed. "I might have said something like that. But I want to know—"

"Do you know who turned you in?" I said.

He hesitated. "I've got a pretty good idea."

I was out on a limb in a lot of ways, with Boo right behind me in unfamiliar territory. If I had to run, I wasn't sure which way to go.

"What would you say if I told you I know who turned you in?"

"How would you know that?"

"My sister and I have friends who like to talk."

"So, tell me."

"Why don't you tell me who *you* think it is, and I'll tell you if you're right."

Boo pointed left. "Driveway is that way."

We climbed the steepest part of the hill, using the trees to propel us onto a gravel-and-sand driveway. I noticed horse droppings and a water trough. I imagined Boo grabbing me and threatening to hold me under until I talked.

Strangely, I didn't feel afraid of Boo. Maybe it was because Ashley had learned some stuff about his past that made him seem a little more human. Or it could have been that he had seemed to care about Tyler and wanted to help.

So I did what a lot of people would call just plain dumb. I decided to tell Boo the truth.

CHAPTER 44

❀ Ashley ❀

The Heckler home was a lot neater than I had expected. It was an open style, and you could see the kitchen and the dining room from the front door. The living room was to the right, and there was a TV and a curved couch. It didn't look like they spent much time there.

There were antique figurines in a glass case by the entry, and family pictures hung on the wall. Boo had a sister Shelly, who had died, and I found a picture showing her on her mother's lap smiling.

Boo's sister Jessie waved shyly at me, and I knew she remembered me from when I'd spoken with her about Boo's past.

"I need the Betadine, Jessie," Mrs. Heckler said with a slight drawl. Tyler was standing, shivering, in the bathtub as she washed his scrapes and tried to clean the leg wound. His brothers stood watching like they'd stumbled onto some reality-TV show.

Mrs. Heckler wasn't what I'd expected either. I thought maybe she'd be dumpy and cross-eyed with bad teeth and arms as long as Boo's, maybe a chain-smoker with tattoos all over. Actually she was pretty with short brown hair, a nice smile, tanned skin that looked silky smooth, and earrings I would have traded my ATV for.

Tyler whimpered as Mrs. Heckler tried to get the dirt and rocks out of his scrapes. It was obvious she knew what she was doing.

"How is he?" I said, introducing myself.

"He'll need stitches," she said.

"Can't you do that?" Raider Hat said. "Ma won't want us taking him to the doctor."

"Listen," she said, her voice stern, "whether you get in trouble for this is not important. Getting your brother medical help is. Got it?"

"Yes, ma'am."

"The piece of wire I took out looked rusty," Mrs. Heckler said. She lifted the cuff of Tyler's pants, and I got a good look at the wound. Too good. It was even worse to look at than Ishmael getting swallowed by Binky. She sighed. "You're going to need a tetanus shot unless you've had one recently."

Tyler looked like he'd been strapped to train tracks while an engine chugged toward him at full speed.

"Where does your mother work?" Mrs. Heckler said.

"I don't know the name of the place," Raider Hat said. "She told us not to call unless it was an emergency."

"Well, this is an emergency. What's the number?"

"It's back at the house on the refrigerator," he said.

Mrs. Heckler asked me to go back to the condo with them and call. "His mother can take him to the doctor's office or the emergency room, but he needs to be seen by someone."

"There goes your trick-or-treating, Tyler," Raider Hat said, making the boy wail.

CHAPTER 45

☻ *Bryce* ☻

I was about to spill the beans to Boo when I heard someone clear his throat. An old man in a straw hat stood there, holding a rifle butt against one leg he had propped on a rock. There was a bulge in his jaw, and he spat a big, brown stream. "Help you, gentlemen?"

Boo told him what had happened, his voice shaking. I'd never seen him like this.

"Kid ran a barb pretty deep in his leg," I said, "and we had to cut a piece of wire off to get him out of your fence."

"That so?"

"Didn't want any of your animals to get out because of it," I said.

He nodded and spat again. "Well, it was good of you to come all this way to tell me." He stared at Boo. "Seen you up here before, haven't I?"

"I don't know. Maybe."

"Well, I'm willing to forget whatever it was you were doing if you'll show me where that break is."

"What did you do?" I said when the man went to get some tools.

"Ever heard of cow tipping?"

"Where you shove them over while they're asleep?"

Boo nodded. "Did that one night back there near the pond. One of them fell in."

I couldn't help but laugh, thinking of Boo running away while a cow splashed in the water.

"The thing drowned."

My smile faded. "You're kidding. That's awful."

"Didn't think anybody saw me, but I guess he did."

Boo stayed with the farmer while he fixed his fence, and I went back to the Heckler house. I hadn't gotten around to telling Boo the truth, but for some reason I wasn't afraid anymore that he would burn down our house.

CHAPTER 46

✖ Ashley ✖

The daredevils' house looked more like I'd expected the Heckler place to look. The sink was full of dirty dishes, the living room had popcorn all over the floor—it looked like no one had vacuumed since the last Olympics—and the phone light blinked with several unanswered messages.

Raider Hat found his mom's work number, and I called her. When I told her that her son had had an accident, she started asking questions just like her sons: Where was he? Was he bleeding? When did it happen? How? All that. She sounded like the most caring mother in the world.

Tyler's mother asked for directions to the Hecklers' and said she was leaving right away.

Raider Hat leaned against the sink. "There goes our life. Mom told us never to go down that hill again." He rummaged in the fridge. "I'm gettin' something to eat."

Eat. I snapped my fingers, and I'm sure the kid thought I was out of my mind. "I have to go back to the Prestons'," I said. "Hope your brother is okay."

CHAPTER 47

☺ *Bryce* ☺

Tyler and his little brother were still at the Hecklers' when I got back.

"That was a nice thing you and your sister did," Mrs. Heckler said with a Texas accent. She was helping Tyler to a chair on the front porch.

"Aaron was a big help," I said.

"Go in and get yourself a drink," she said. "I made lemonade."

I found the kitchen and poured a glass. It tasted freshly squeezed. I saw a hallway. If I ever wanted to explore the place, now was my chance.

I figured there were bedrooms upstairs, but there were also two downstairs. The first had a king-sized bed, so that must have been the parents'. At the back of the house, I twisted a doorknob and felt as if I were entering a wild animal's lair. All the fear I had of Boo Heckler rushed through me. I expected to see shrunken heads, animal skins, or maybe Boo's hit list. Instead, it looked like any other kid's room—mine even.

A small desk in the corner was strewn with schoolbooks and a couple of notebooks. By Boo's bedside was a nightstand, the only thing in the room even mildly clean. A picture of his family, including the little sister who had died, faced his pillow. Under the picture lay a Bible, and I raised my eyebrows at that one. I couldn't imagine Boo doing devotions. Beside that was a book from Juicy Pages, a local bookstore and juice bar run by our old principal.

The more I looked, the more curious I became. It was like coming upon the ruins of an ancient civilization you'd always wondered about, and now the clues were right at your fingertips.

"You found the lemonade?" Mrs. Heckler said.

I almost dropped my glass. "Yes. Sorry. I always wondered what Boo's—uh, Aaron's—room was like."

Mrs. Heckler stepped inside, as if giving me permission to stay. "He talks about you and your sister a lot. I'm glad I finally got to meet you."

"What does he say?"

She walked to the bed and straightened the covers, talking as she tugged and tucked. "At first all he could talk about was those four-wheelers of yours. He said you were going to let him bring them home one weekend so he could ride around here."

"Really," I said, more as a statement than a question.

"He has classes with your sister this year. He says she's nice. That they talk a lot."

I didn't nod or even breathe. I got the feeling Mrs. Heckler didn't believe her son any more than I would have, and I knew the truth.

"What's it really like for him at school?" Mrs. Heckler said. "I've talked with his teachers and the principal and assistant principal and just about everyone you can talk with."

I took a breath. "Last year he . . . well, he had some friends, but they weren't that good. This year, since those kids have moved on, he spends a lot more time alone."

"So he doesn't have many friends."

I shrugged. "He seems angry most of the time. I haven't ever seen him laugh. And he can be mean to people."

She nodded and looked at the picture by Boo's bed. "We've tried. . . . He's really not a bad person, Bryce. He's been through some difficult things."

Mrs. Heckler didn't know I knew that Boo had been there when her daughter was killed, that he was responsible for Shelley being there, that Mrs. Heckler and her husband were having trouble. And she didn't know Ashley and I had told the police about Boo's vandalism spree that sent him to the juvenile detention center.

"I guess him going to juvie didn't help things," I said.

"I'm not sure. Part of me thinks it knocked some sense into him. Another part thinks he may do something worse and wind up . . ."

She didn't have to finish the sentence, because I had thought the same thing. You wondered if you'd see his picture on one of those most-wanted TV shows someday.

"Bryce, I want to ask you a favor. You don't have to say yes. You don't have to say anything. Just think about it." She ran her hand over the bedspread. "Would you consider being Aaron's friend?"

CHAPTER 48

❀ Ashley ❀

Every time I looked at Bailey, that dog seemed to be telling me something with his big, brown eyes.

I only had to look at the kitchen table to realize he was apologizing. The centerpiece with the flowers was on the floor in a hundred pieces. The salt and pepper shakers were wood—thankfully. The napkin holder was on the floor too. I picked up the pieces of pottery and threw them away along with the flowers.

When I had everything back to normal, I realized the box with the rat in it was missing. I'd seen Bryce put it on the table when he ran inside. Had he taken it upstairs?

I ran to Binky's room and found the snake more agitated than ever. It was like he'd had his salad the night before and was waiting for the main course (but I'm no snake expert).

The rat box was nowhere in sight, so I went back downstairs. Bailey scratched at the door, so I put him on his leash outside and came back in. I gasped when I saw the torn-up box on the living-room floor. The rat was long gone, and the box had been chewed into more pieces than the flower vase.

Do dogs eat rats?

I searched under every table, chair, and couch. I even pulled the refrigerator away from the wall a little and shined a flashlight underneath and behind.

I sat with my back against the kitchen wall and promised myself I would never watch any pets again as long as I lived.

CHAPTER 49

☺ *Bryce* ☺

Mrs. Heckler didn't know what she was asking. Becoming friends with Boo was like signing your own death warrant. A verse in Proverbs says it's important to choose good friends. But the way she looked at me with pleading eyes made it clear she thought this might be Boo's last chance for life outside prison.

"I know you're a Christian and that your family is strong," she said.

How does she know that?

"I'm not naive enough to think you'll want to spend a lot of time together. You have different interests. I saw the article about you and the bike ride earlier this summer."

"Aaron likes fixing cars. I could probably get into that."

A look of hope came over her face, and she talked faster. "I can't help thinking that just one good friend could turn things around for him. The people he's been drawn to since we moved here haven't been good for him."

I've heard stories of mean kids growing up and becoming preachers. I have a pretty good imagination, but I couldn't see Boo becoming a Billy Graham or pastoring a church someday, telling people about God.

My friend Jeff Alexander had really lived life to the fullest. On our bike trip he said something I'll never forget. Jeff said the big question for him about school and life in general was to figure out whether the world is going to change you or if you're going to change the world. "The trick is figuring out what you really believe and living it out," he said. "Then you can handle all the peer pressure."

I stared at Mrs. Heckler. "My sister and I have asked Aaron to come to our youth group. He wasn't interested."

"Ask him again. Sometimes it takes a few times for him to let down and—"

"What are you doing in my room?" Boo said.

"Aaron," his mother said. She ran her hand over the bedspread again. What is it with moms and bedspreads, anyway? My mom does the same thing. You'd think life can't go on unless a bed is made. "Bryce and I were just talking about you."

Boo gave me a look, then glanced back at his mom. "There's a car coming up the driveway."

CHAPTER 50

✖ Ashley ✖

There was no rat to be found. Bailey barked on the patio, and
when I went to get him I saw a woman on a bench near the swings.
The morning fog and clouds had disappeared, but the afternoon sun
was in a hiding mode, and the wind had picked up. Funny that
someone would sit outside on a day like this.

It wasn't until I got near her that I realized it was the woman
from Mr. Bookman's house. She looked about the same age as him,
maybe a little younger, and she had puffy eyes. Probably all that late-
night stuff with the phone. She smiled.

"Sorry to bother you," I said, "but you didn't happen to see a rat run by here, did you?"

She frowned. "They have rat trouble around here?"

"No, it was a pet—actually food for a snake."

"Oh," she said, sitting up straighter. "You're watching the animals. You ride the ATVs."

I nodded and held out a hand. "I'm Ashley."

Usually grown-ups like it when you look them in the eye and offer to shake their hands. But she ignored my hand and pointed at me. "I don't want to catch you riding around here tonight with all the little kids out. Those things are more dangerous than you know."

She stood and headed toward Mr. Bookman's condo. "Bad things happen to kids who ride those," she said over her shoulder.

Was that a warning or a threat?

CHAPTER 51

☺ *Bryce* ☺

When I told Ashley about my conversation with Mrs. Heckler, she said, "Bryce, this is great. You become his friend, and we can keep an eye on him all the time."

I stared at her. "Why don't we stick with the original plan of you dating him? That way you two can get close, go to dances—"

The look on her face stopped me. She pointed. "There it goes!"

I turned to see the rat's tail slither under the door to Binky's room and flew after it. When I got inside, there was no sign of the thing. "Maybe we should just let Binky out and let him find Mr. Rat."

"Don't even kid about that," Ashley said. "All we need is to lose

Binky down some heating vent to the furnace where he gets cooked just before the Prestons come back."

"Look under the bed. I'll check the closet."

Ashley gave me one of her girl looks, like I'd just asked her to make me a rat sandwich with cheese. She's good about some gross stuff, like cleaning out the alpaca barn, but other things turn her stomach. I could tell she didn't want to be looking under the bed when Mr. Rat ran for his life.

"We have him trapped in here, right?" she said. "Then let's make sure he stays in here." She got a couple of towels, closed the bedroom door, and stuffed the towels under the space at the bottom. Then she went to the other side of the room by the window. "I'll watch and tell you if he's on the move."

I rolled my eyes. "Ashley, you act like a girl at the weirdest times."

CHAPTER 52

✖ Ashley ✖

Bryce could complain all he wanted, but I was done with the rat hunt. Sometimes you just have to draw the line. I stood on a chair where I could keep an eye on the bed, the closet, and any other place the thing could scurry.

I was also right by the window and could see the first trick-or-treaters making their way to the neighborhood. There were the usual ghosts, goblins, and witches, with a few Scooby-Doos and Supermen thrown in. All had candy bags—some from the grocery store. Others looked expensive. The outfits ranged from a sheet over the head with holes cut out for eyes to full-fledged Spidermen complete with Silly String web makers.

Something moved in my peripheral vision, and I looked past Mr. Harper's condo to the garage. The door was rising on the first bay. Our chance to see what kind of car was in there.

I jumped down from my chair and ran into the hall.

"What?" Bryce said, but I closed the door behind me and pulled the towels through to make sure no rat got out.

I bounded all the way down the stairs, out the front door, and past the Preston condo, through the pine trees at the edge of the courtyard, and into Mr. Harper's side yard. Whatever car had pulled out of there had gone the other way, and the garage door was on its way down. I raced to the garage to get a closer look. The door was about two feet from closing when I focused on something gray on the concrete at the back of the garage.

If I stuck my foot under there, it might go back up, but it shut tight before I could reach it.

I ran across the road, past Mr. Harper's condo, and through the courtyard. On the other side of the complex I pulled up, panting.

The car was nowhere in sight.

CHAPTER 53

☻ *Bryce* ☻

As soon as Ashley closed the door, Mr. Rat bolted from under the bed and rushed headlong into the closet. I dived for him, but he moved like lightning, his little feet scampering over the carpeted floor like he was in a race for his life—which he was. I grabbed one of the towels from under the door, opened the closet, and prepared to throw it on him, but all kinds of shoes, boxes, and paper littered the floor.

To my left Snooks sat up in his box, sniffing the air, trying to figure out what was going on, I guess. I put the top over him and told him not to watch.

I spotted Mr. Rat behind a box, moved to trap him, and bunched the towel on the other end. I pushed the box closer, and Mr. Rat tried to high-jump the towel. I struggled to keep him under it. He made another effort, and I yelled and covered him. I wondered if Mr. Rat prayed for one more chance, but rats don't have souls. I pictured him reading *The Purpose-Driven Rat*, and that made me smile.

A lump moved under the towel, so I pounced. I wrapped the thing, brought him to Binky's cage, and lifted the top. Binky looked at me with hungry eyes, and I figured I'd better give him something quick or he'd come after *me*. I opened the towel, but nothing dropped. Mr. Rat was clinging to two threads of the towel. I shook it, and he finally plopped into the cage. I slammed the top shut, and Binky went into high gear, surrounding the rat and giving him a squeeze.

When Ashley came back, I put the towel over the cage to spare her. "Mission accomplished," I said.

The doorbell rang, and Bailey barked from his tether in the backyard. We raced downstairs and found a Grim Reaper, a Darth Vader, a Freddy Krueger, and a Cinderella at the door. *Impressive quartet.*

"Trick or treat!" the four screamed.

Ashley plopped mini candy bars into their bags.

"Thank you!" they said, surveying their take.

As if on cue, a mist rolled in from the mountain, and a cloud shrouded the town like a dark-gloved hand.

Ashley told me what she'd seen by the garage. In Mr. Harper's condo a light flickered from the television.

"Probably a decoy," I said. "I'll bet he's out wreaking havoc on fast-food restaurants right now."

"How would he have recorded those bits from the movies? You know how old people are with technology."

The doorbell rang, and this time three lightsaber-laden boys stood there. I recognized the Morris boys—their father was right behind them. He owns the alpaca farm.

The boys recognized us and squealed, "Trick or treat!"—dipping their sabers to say hello. All three were Jedi, and the youngest looked like Yoda.

Ashley and I gave them extra candy.

When they were gone, I said, "Get your jacket and let's take Bailey for a walk. See what we can see."

The doorbell rang again, and this time it was only one little Batman with drooping ears. He held a canvas bag with the name *Dylan* on it.

"We don't need Bailey," I said.

CHAPTER 54

✖ Ashley ✖

I told Mom she could pick up Dylan in an hour or two.

Bryce wrote a note that said *Please take three pieces* and put the candy outside the door.

"Think anybody will stick by that?" I said.

Bryce shrugged. "When it's gone, it's gone."

Dylan pretended to fly, with his black cape flapping in the breeze. Pine needles and aspen leaves spread over the landscape. Tiny drops of water hit me as I faced the wind. Flurries mixed with ice. I pointed toward the next condo, but Dylan had already moved to Mrs. Waldorf's. She laughed at Dylan's outfit.

"Our little brother," I said.

"Well, aren't you a big superhero! I'll bet you have to have a lot of candy to give you energy, don't you?"

Dylan gave her a wide-eyed nod.

She shoved three Life Savers suckers into his bag and said, "Be careful out there tonight, Batman, and take care of your brother and sister."

Some families go all out when it comes to Halloween—pumpkin candles hanging from trees, spiderwebs on the eaves. Others boycott it and hand out Christian literature to trick-or-treaters. As we walked down the sidewalk, a light flickered from Mr. Harper's back window. The garage door was still closed. I pushed Dylan up his steps, sure no one would come to the door.

Dylan could just reach the doorbell, adjusting his mask.

The door suddenly opened. Mr. Harper held a huge bowl of candy and smiled. "Well, this looks like little Bryce!"

"I'm Dylan!"

"Aren't you something!" he said, laughing.

From inside I recognized the theme song to a famous Western movie. Mr. Harper said, "I was just watching John Wayne try and get the bad guys. You kids have a good night."

"Didn't you just leave a few minutes ago?" I said.

"Had to run out for more candy."

Bryce glanced at me as we walked away. "Must have gone through the express drive-thru this time. Maybe somebody borrowed his car. Or maybe that's not his garage."

Dylan ran through the crowd down the sidewalk to the next condo.

"Oh no," Bryce said. "He's at Mr. Bookman's!"

CHAPTER 55

☺ *Bryce* ☺

I tried to reach Dylan before he rang the doorbell, but Mr. Bookman was already standing there. He handed Dylan one package of Smarties and an individually wrapped Twizzlers.

Dylan looked inside his bag and sighed.

"What do you say, buddy?" I said.

"Thank you."

"Ah, Bruce and Annette," Mr. Bookman said, stepping onto the porch. "Is this a future Red Rock middle schooler?"

"Sure is," I said. "This is Dylan."

He patted Batman on the head and looked at Ashley. "I understand you had a conversation with Stephanie this afternoon."

Ashley paused. "Oh, in the courtyard? Yes, I sure did."

"We're both concerned about the ATVs. Her emotions are a little raw at the moment, and she probably came across strong. I'm sure you'll be sensitive to her feelings."

"We only ride them when we have to—," I said.

Ashley grabbed my arm. "We don't want to upset anyone," she said.

More trick-or-treaters came up behind us, and we helped Dylan down the steps. We met a kid dressed as Elvis and a little Count Dracula. Elvis had two candy bags, which was weird. The kids looked at us like we were supposed to recognize them.

"Iss uss," the count said through his fake teeth.

Tyler's brothers.

"How's Tyler doing?"

"He's home giving out candy," Elvis said. "I'm collecting for him, but I have to explain and it's kind of a pain."

"You're a good brother," I said. "You guys be careful."

"No kidding! A guy in an old car just about ran over us a while ago."

"What did he look like?" Bryce said.

"Not sure. He came barreling out of this road, and I had to jump out of the way so fast I didn't get a good look. But his face looked strange."

"Like he was wearing a mask?" I said.

"Yeah, like that. An adult trick-or-treating."

CHAPTER 56

✖ Ashley ✖

$\mathcal{B}$ryce and I tried to convince Dylan that we needed to go back to the Prestons' right away. I told him if he caught a cold he wouldn't be able to eat his candy, and he'd have to go to the doctor and get a shot. "Maybe three or four shots."

He just waved his bat arms and flew along the sidewalk, calling out, "Batman's not scared of doctors!"

"You can go back if you want, Bryce," I said. "I'll watch him."

Bryce scowled. "Hey, Dylan, you want some hot chocolate?"

Dylan turned, his bat ears flopping and his eyes wide. "As soon as we do 100 houses!"

I complain about Dylan a lot. He leaves the toilet seat up and has bad aim. He chases Pippin and Frodo through the yard in his superhero costumes, and he's probably taken years off their lives. He cries and whines, has Mom fill his cereal bowl and then doesn't eat it, spills milk, wakes me up on Saturdays when I'm trying to sleep in, and a lot of other things that get on my nerves.

But I have to admit that watching Dylan walk and laugh and get in his own little world is one of the best things in my life. When he pulls out his CD collection (about four CDs) and puts on his headphones and sings along, I think I'm going to die. I gave him one of my favorite CDs and he memorized the words in less than an hour, then kept playing it over and over and singing along with it. I hate to think what our lives would be like without the little guy.

Still, I was cold and really wanted to find out more about Mr. Harper. Did he have a reason for leaving so fast that he almost ran over the daredevils? Was he really wearing a mask, or was that the boy's imagination—or Bryce's suggestion?

I used to think there was nothing good about houses being close together, but I forgot about trick-or-treating. Black clouds engulfed the sky, and the wind picked up. My fingers didn't feel like part of my body anymore. Ditto for my nose and toes. The spits of snow and sleet turned into a driving wall of bad weather.

"Getting cold, Dylan?" I said as he raced up another driveway.

"Not yet!"

A young mom looked out, went crazy over Dylan's outfit, and dumped a handful of candy in his bag.

The driveway at the next house was sloped, and going up was treacherous. Dylan just got off the driveway into the crunchy, cold grass to the door while Bryce and I slipped and slid.

It turned out to be the home of a lady from our church, and she invited us in. Dylan wanted to keep going until he got a look at the candy in her pumpkin bowl.

We stood by the cozy fireplace and let the feeling come back into our hands and feet. She brought a tray of hot-chocolate mugs, and we wrapped our hands around them.

Bryce pulled out his cell phone to dial Mom, afraid she was on her way to the Prestons' to pick up Dylan. His battery was dead, so he used the house phone. Mom said to stay where we were and she'd pick us up.

The doorbell rang and Dylan jumped. He asked if he could give out some candy, and the woman nodded. He put one piece in everyone's bag, then turned and smiled like he'd passed a major test in life.

From the TV, a man with a deep voice said, "We have a breaking story on this Halloween night of yet another robbery at a fast-food restaurant, this time north of Colorado Springs in the Glen Eagle area."

Just south of us.

CHAPTER 57

☺ *Bryce* ☺

"It seems children aren't the only ones with the tricks tonight," the anchorman said. "If you see the vehicle described or have any information, call the number on your screen. . . ."

Ashley wrote the number and stuffed it in her pocket. "Think we should call and tell them what we know?"

I shook my head. "I can't believe Mr. Harper did this. For all we know, it could be Mrs. Waldorf. All that stuff she's burying is money from her heists."

"Come on, Bryce."

"Think about it. It could be a female. The robber never speaks."

"I guess we need more information before we call anybody."

I nodded. "Just wanted to hear you say it."

Lights shone on the living-room wall and brought back a memory of our real dad coming home from work. One of my favorite memories was of him walking through the snow, coming into the house, and gathering us in his arms. Funny, it takes only some lights or a song or the smell of my dad's old cologne to bring back those visions.

Mom showed up wrapped in a winter coat, shivering. Dylan thought she was a trick-or-treater and cried when he couldn't give her candy, a sure sign it was time to put Batman to bed.

"The roads are really bad," Mom said. "I saw a couple of accidents."

CHAPTER 58

❦ Ashley ❦

I almost fell when we walked outside. The temperature had dropped to freezing. Perfect football weather, terrible for kids running around the neighborhood for candy.

The only kids still outside were the diehards—the Halloweenies. They wore the ugliest costumes—hideous masks and fake blood. They would never take an umbrella, were soaked to the bone, and their face paint had long ago run and faded. They knew that once the little kids gave up, there was an endless supply of candy and parents ready to unload it awaiting them.

Pine needles had ice forming on their ends and sparkled in our headlights. Mom drove slowly back to the Prestons', keeping an eye out for kids. She asked if we wanted her to come in, and Bryce and I rolled our eyes.

"Aren't you going to count it with me?" Dylan said. He had a kindergarten assignment to count all his candy and write down the different types.

"Maybe tomorrow," I said.

Dylan wailed, "But you promised."

"It's okay," Mom said. "I'll get Batman to bed, and you can come home for lunch and keep your promise tomorrow."

Bryce picked up the candy basket as I put the key in the door. "Well, what do you know?" he said. "It's empty."

The house was dark and quiet. Something rattled downstairs, and I jumped.

"Just the furnace," Bryce said.

I willed myself not to be scared, though it rattled like a train engine. Then it stopped and everything was quiet.

"Something's wrong," I said.

Bryce looked out the window. "TV's still flickering at Mr. Harper's."

"No, in here." Then I remembered. "Bailey! I left him outside!"

CHAPTER 59

◓ *Bryce* ◓

Ashley and I rushed out and found Bailey's leash hanging from the wire, swaying in the wind. Ice had formed on the wire.

"He's gone," Ashley said. "I let Fred escape, I killed the fish, nearly starved the snake, and now the dog's been sto—"

A brilliant white light flashed, and she jumped back. It was as if someone were taking a picture of us. Then an earsplitting crack of thunder shook the ground.

We raced back inside. You don't see rain, sleet, and snow mixed with lightning and thunder that often, and believe me, you don't want to. This would send even the Halloweenies running inside.

But outside, the two healthy daredevils were hanging around near the swings.

"Those kids are going to get killed," I said.

"Their parents should have had cats instead," Ashley said. "Hey, maybe Bailey just got loose and is trying to get back here. We should look for him."

"You've watched *Homeward Bound* too many times," I said.

With another brilliant flash, the lights went out, and thunder boomed. It got so quiet you could almost hear a rat digesting.

The phone in the living room chirped.

"That phone's not electric?" Ashley said as we felt our way there.

I reached the couch, then the coffee table, and finally the little table that held a lamp, a flower vase (which I knocked off), and the phone.

Ashley was right behind me and grabbed it. Lightning flashed again, and I saw her face scrunch up. She covered the mouthpiece and whispered, "Somebody's on the line."

I took the phone. Someone was breathing on the other end. Labored. Wheezy. The hair on the back of my neck stood so at attention it could have said, "Sir, yes sir" and dropped to the floor for 20 push-ups.

"Hello?" I said, my voice cracking. I cleared my throat and said it again with authority, like a man—a man with hair on the back of his neck standing up.

No response. Just more breathing and wheezing.

I pushed the hang-up button, then released it. No dial tone . . . just the wheezing.

Then the line went dead.

Dial tone.

I didn't want to tell Ashley what I thought. I didn't want to scare her.

"What?" she said.

No sense keeping it from her. I whispered, "It could have been someone on an extension in here."

CHAPTER 60

❀ Ashley ❀

There's nothing scarier than thinking a person is in your house, except maybe knowing a snake is loose in your bedroom.

"Who could it be?" I whispered.

"Boo?"

"You *told* him we're staying here?"

"Shh. *You* wanted me to be his friend." Bryce moved to the living room and looked out the back window. "Power's out in the rest of the neighborhood."

Silhouetted in the occasional flash of lightning, the condos and houses in the distance looked haunted.

Bryce went back to the front door, where he'd dropped the flash-light. That little stream of light somehow calmed me a bit.

We heard a big dog and assumed it was Bailey. Rushing out the front door, we had to grab each other and struggle to stay standing as soon as we hit the sidewalk. It was slicker than whale blubber. We made it to Mrs. Waldorf's door and knocked. More barking.

"Maybe it was Bailey on the phone," Bryce said. I don't know how he can be so light at times like this, but that's my brother.

"Whoever it was had a wheeze," I said, "like they have asthma."

"Maybe it was Fred calling from Florida."

I punched Bryce on the arm.

"Fred could have caught a cold," he said.

Mrs. Waldorf peeked out and hesitated until Bryce turned the flashlight on our faces. "Oh, it's you two," she said. Candles lit her living room. "Bailey looked cold, so I brought him in here."

"Thanks," I said. "That's a relief. Have you noticed anybody near the Prestons' place tonight?"

She scratched her head. "No, I don't think so. Something wrong?"

"We just got a weird phone call," I said.

On her kitchen table sat another plastic bag, glinting in the candlelight.

"Was Bailey barking? How'd you notice him?"

"He was being quiet as a mouse, poor thing."

A car zoomed up to the garage, and Bryce gave me a look. "We should get Bailey back to the house. Thanks, Mrs. Waldorf."

CHAPTER 61

☺ *Bryce* ☺

Ashley gripped Bailey's collar as we rushed to the garage. We hopped over the slick sidewalk onto the grass. Bailey almost jackknifed, pawing at the ice like a cartoon character.

I turned the flashlight off before we passed Mr. Harper's condo. The garage door had already come down, but we could hear footsteps on the pavement.

"I'll be right back," I said, handing Ashley the flashlight.

I sprinted in front of the buildings, behind the little bus-stop shed, and to the next set of condos.

A man cursed, and I heard him fall. He picked himself up, climbed the steps, and went inside the drummer's condo.

I ran back and told Ashley what I'd seen. Having Bailey with us made us both feel safer as we listened in the cold night air.

"The robber could be the drummer," I whispered. "I didn't see which garage he parked in."

"Me either," Ashley said. "But we have another suspect." She told me about the plastic bag she'd seen at Mrs. Waldorf's. "Plus, she said Bailey didn't bark."

"So?"

"How would she have seen him if she didn't go outside? She had to go past the back patio, and that leads right to the garage. Her shoes were wet."

Bailey tried to pull away from Ashley. She let him go and he scratched on the Prestons' front door until we opened it. He ran to the kitchen and scarfed down the rest of his food. Then he burped. We took him through the whole house, searching every room, every closet, every bathroom. Ashley found candles in the dining room, and I got matches from the pantry. Soon we had the coffee table lined with five candles, and I was surprised how much light they gave off.

"You know what would taste good right now?" Ashley said. "Popcorn."

"Great, but there's no power."

She groaned. "I never thought of all the things you can't do without electricity. No TV. No DVDs."

"No heat for the fish."

She gasped. "How long will it take for them to . . . you know . . . go belly-up?"

"Probably overnight." I turned on the gas fireplace, which was near the fish tank. That might give them a little warmth, and anyway, how often do fish get to see fire? Maybe it was a treat.

Someone knocked at the door.

CHAPTER 62

❉ Ashley ❉

I was already jumpy, and when Bailey barked and ran into the room, I wanted to blow the candles out and hide under the couch. I grabbed Bailey's collar. The big dog was a comfort, my own personal police officer with shaggy hair and big teeth.

Bryce opened the door slowly and flicked on the flashlight. Elvis was back in the building. He had a weird look, not to mention those sideburns and the white jumpsuit.

"Mom asked me to bring you this," he said, holding out a basket of candy. There were 20 mini 3 Musketeers bars, a hundred Tootsie Rolls, and several rolls of taffy, all from the Prestons' basket.

"Mom said to bring it over and say we're sorry we caused so much trouble."

"Is Tyler going to be okay?" I said.

"They gave him a tennis shot—or something like that. Said he's going to be sore for a while. They had to scrub all his scrapes out, and Mom said he hollered a lot. They don't want him to get an injection or something." He turned to leave.

"Hey," I said, "listen. When you said that car almost ran you over, are you sure the driver was wearing a mask? Could it have been someone with a lot of wrinkles?"

Elvis shrugged. "Could have been. It was dark. I was just trying to get out of the way."

I felt the hair stiffen on the back of Bailey's neck, and he strained to look past Elvis toward the pine trees. He growled that deep, guttural, big-throated growl you hear in movies when a dog is about to tear someone apart.

"Guess I'd better go," Elvis said. He slid down the sidewalk as Bryce pointed his flashlight into the darkness.

The light hit two eyes. He was dressed in black, as if trying to be Zorro, but the costume was all wrong. He was at least a foot taller than most trick-or-treaters, and a white pillowcase dangled in front of him. Fake blood dripped from his mouth.

Bryce whispered, "Boo."

CHAPTER 63

◔ *Bryce* ◔

Boo walked toward us with a smirk. I was surprised to see him alone, wet, and shivering.

"Watch the sidewalk," I said.

Boo waved as if it was no problem; then his feet flew out from under him and he landed with a thud. Somehow he kept his candy from hitting the ground. He looked ridiculous, but I wasn't about to laugh.

I hurried out and helped him up while Ashley took the growling, barking Bailey downstairs and locked him in the bathroom. He scratched on the door, but Ashley yelled at him and banged on it until he quit.

I took the candy Elvis had brought back and dumped it into Boo's pillowcase.

"So, how's it going tonight?" Ashley asked, coming back upstairs.

Boo shrugged. "I'm gettin' lots of the stuff nobody wants. Plus I'm beatin' up a lot of little kids and stealing their candy bags."

Ashley frowned at him.

"He's kidding," I said. "Aren't you?"

It was the closest I've ever seen Boo come to genuinely laughing. "Yeah, I try not to beat up kids on the weekend."

"So," Ashley said, "you want to come in? We've got a fire going."

Boo peeked inside the dark house. "Actually I want to talk with your brother."

"Me?" I said, my voice cracking.

"I'll go downstairs and see about Bailey," Ashley said. "No problem."

Boo stepped in and let his candy bag thunk on the tile floor. He smelled like a wet dog, and his black coat dripped. He sat on the couch and it creaked. All I could think of was what his clothes were going to do to the leather. His face glowed eerily in the candlelight. Boo was scary enough in the daylight.

"So," I said, "what brings you all the way over here—?"

"What you said today. You know who got me sent to juvie."

I tried to sit still. It's one thing to face a bully in the daylight when you can at least run, but it's another in the dark when his face is plastered with blood and black makeup.

"Did you call here a while ago?" I said.

Boo frowned. "Why would I do that? I don't even know the number." He put his hands behind his head. "Just tell me who it was."

"What're you going to do to them?"

"*Them?* There's more than one?"

"I meant *them* in the . . . you know, the collective kind of . . . well . . . you know . . . inclusive way, not the plural."

"Huh?"

I scratched my head and shifted. "I don't want to tell you because I know what you'll do to him."

"So it is a *him.*" Boo sat forward. "I knew it."

"Why don't you just forget it? You don't have to get revenge."

"You don't know what it's like in juvie. He made my life a night-mare. He had no right. I was just having a little fun, and nobody would have caught me if that Duncan Swift hadn't ratted me out."

My heart stopped, and the air went out of the room. "Why do you think it was him?"

"He lives close to me. I've seen him in the woods looking, spy-ing." Boo stood quickly, dripping on the floor. "I can probably catch him outside. I saw him with a couple of his friends earlier."

Duncan was a good athlete and could probably hold his own with just about anybody else, but Boo was a lot taller and weighed more. "Aaron," I said, "sit down."

"No time." He reached for the door.

"It wasn't Duncan."

"Yeah, right."

"No, I mean it. I swear he's not the one."

"Then who?" He opened the door and turned back, staring at me.

Then it hit me. Duncan's house wasn't near Boo's. It was on the other side of town. But Boo knew we were friends. He knew I wouldn't want Duncan to get hurt. I could breathe again.

Boo just stood there, waiting.

Ashley appeared at the top of the stairs. "Wait, Aaron," she said. "I'll tell you who it was."

CHAPTER 64

❀ Ashley ❀

I'd had a crush on Bryce's friend for a long time, but Duncan acted like I didn't exist. Maybe after Boo got finished with Bryce and me, Duncan would visit me in the hospital.

"Ash, I don't think—"

"You can't let Duncan hang for this," I said. "Aaron, Duncan was *not* the one who ratted on you. It was—"

"She's right," Bryce said. "Besides, you're just trying to trick us. Duncan doesn't live anywhere near you."

Boo ping-ponged between Bryce and me, staring like Franken-stein's monster, his eyes flickering in the candlelight. "You put the note in my locker, didn't you?" he said finally.

"Note?" Bryce said a little too late.

Boo narrowed his eyes. "Who are you trying to protect? And why were you all chummy with my mom, checking out my bedroom?" He pointed at me. "And my little sister said you came to our house. Got up in the tree house and asked a bunch of questions about our family."

"What's wrong with talking to your sister?" I said.

Boo chewed the inside of his cheek and breathed through his nose, snorting like a bull about to charge. Then he looked past me to the window. "What—?"

Someone in the courtyard had a flashlight trained on the ground. The person was digging with a small shovel.

"You thinking what I'm thinking?" Bryce said.

"Yes," I said, "if you're thinking that's Mrs. Waldorf burying the cash."

Bryce turned to Boo. "We'll have to finish this later."

"What's going on?" he said.

"We may have just solved the fast-food robberies."

Boo looked blank, like he hadn't heard anything about that. "Well, I'm not leaving until I get an answer."

"Suit yourself," Bryce said. "We'll be back."

CHAPTER 65

☺ *Bryce* ☺

Ashley let Bailey out of the bathroom downstairs. Then Boo followed us outside, our breath white in the air. The freezing drizzle was still coming, but we were sheltered by the pine trees. Mrs. Waldorf started humming or singing.

Boo just stared. "That's a strange old lady. What's wrong with her?"

The way Boo said it almost made me laugh. He drawled, like his mother.

"Look," he said, "I'll get out of here if you just tell me who it was that—"

"Both times there have been robberies," I said, "she's been back here with a plastic bag. It might be the cash, but we're not sure."

"How long have you known this old bird?"

"Just a few days. She lives right over there."

Boo studied her like the engine of an old car. "She seem like the type who would rob a restaurant?"

"Not really, but you never know."

"I got an idea," Boo said. "Let me go find out what she's doing. If you two accuse her of stealing something and she turns out to be just a crazy old bat, she'll probably go weird on you. I'll pretend I'm trick-or-treating and see if I can get a look at whatever that is."

"What if it's money?" I said.

"They'll probably offer some kind of ree-ward," Boo said. "We'll split it three ways."

"No, I mean what if she starts swinging that shovel at you?"

"I'm not much into sports, but I can outrun an old lady with a shovel. Get ready to call the cops." He went back inside and got his candy-filled pillowcase.

Life sure takes some interesting twists and turns, but this topped them all. Boo Heckler a partner in an investigation. He loped across the courtyard with his sopping pillowcase over his shoulder, looking like Christian in *The Pilgrim's Progress,* except for the black outfit, stringy hair, and fake blood.

Boo approached Mrs. Waldorf, pulled the pillowcase from his shoulder, and placed it on the ground. He said something, and then she motioned to her condo. I imagined she said her candy was inside. Boo waved like it didn't matter.

"What would you give for a recording of this conversation?" Ashley said.

I shook my head. "Ten percent of whatever's in those bags."

"Have you heard anything about a reward?"

"You mean a ree-ward?" I said. "No."

Then I started providing the dialogue for what we wished we could hear. "That's okay, Mrs. Waldorf. I got enough chocolate in here to feed a small village."

"I don't have any candy," Ashley said, cackling. "But would you like some money?"

"Sure, but I only take 10s and 20s."

We watched as Mrs. Waldorf pointed at the ground.

Boo leaned over to inspect the hole, which looked deep. Suddenly he snapped bolt upright, slowly raised his head, and looked at her. He stepped back and pointed.

Mrs. Waldorf held out both hands, like she was pleading her case.

Boo slung his candy sack over his shoulder and took another step back. He looked at us and shook his head. Then he turned and ran into the night.

CHAPTER 66

✖ Ashley ✖

"At least we don't have to deal with all of Boo's questions," Bryce said. "Looks like he's headed home."

Mrs. Waldorf picked up the plastic bag with a grunt and put it in the ground. Then she covered it over and smoothed out the dirt with her shovel before going back inside.

I wondered how long it would take for the power company to get the electricity on again. As I opened the Prestons' patio door, Bailey bounded out and ran past us through the pine trees. We both shouted at him, but the dog looked like he'd been planning his break all along. *Maybe he's going after Fred.* I heard his snort and pant echo off the condos.

"Grab the leash," Bryce said. "I'll get the flashlight."

We looked for him in the courtyard, near the garage, and even down the road. Then Bryce heard him panting and scratching, and we ran behind Mr. Harper's condo. We found a deep hole Bailey had dug but nothing in it.

We caught sight of him at the Prestons' back patio, but by the time we got there he was gone again.

"He's going to get hit by a car," I said.

"Pity the car."

We passed where Boo and Mrs. Waldorf had talked. Bryce groaned when he aimed the flashlight at the ground. It was covered with dirt, but everywhere I'd seen a mound there was now an empty hole. No plastic bags.

We kept looking, using the only flashlight we had. We finally went to the drummer's condo, thinking maybe Bailey had smelled another dog there. But the drummer kept such odd hours that we doubted he had a pet, other than maybe an owl.

To my surprise, Bailey looked at us from the front porch of the man's condo. Bryce pointed the flashlight, and Bailey's eyes glowed red, sending a shiver down my back. His coat was covered in mud.

"Come on, boy," Bryce whispered. He snapped his fingers. "Come over here."

"I'll get him," I said.

I headed for the steps, and Bailey dipped his head to the concrete and moved to the end of the porch. As if I didn't exist, he began to sniff and lick at the bottom of a barbecue grill. *Just like a guy. Uninterested in the person who cares for him most.*

I tried to coax him out, but the grill must have been a lot more interesting.

Bryce pointed the flashlight just ahead of me, and the railing cast an eerie shadow.

Then I saw it.

A man's face in the window.

I yelped.

The drummer stepped out.

"I was just trying to get the dog," I said, hands shaking.

"It's okay. Don't freak. He probably smelled the burgers I cooked yesterday." He waved at Bryce. "Your power out too?"

"For a while now."

"I was playing a gig at a local place and everything went black. They couldn't light candles because of some ordinance, but it wouldn't have done us any good. All the other instruments use electricity, so we were out of business."

"We've heard you play," I said. "You're good."

"Thanks. If you know anybody who wants lessons, tell them about me." He handed me a card.

I said, "We have lots of friends at the middle school who might love drum lessons."

"Yeah," he said. "The principal there lives next door. Miles is a good guy."

It was weird hearing Mr. Bookman called by his first name. "Right, we know him well. Except I didn't know he was married— or has a girlfriend."

"Oh, that's his sister. She moved in a couple of weeks ago. Sold her place up in Steamboat Springs. Miles never has a problem with my practicing—I think he wears earplugs at night. And she works in the night anyway."

"Yeah, I see a light on over there at all hours."

"Right. You ever see those infomercials on TV late at night? She

takes phone calls from people buying exercise machines, hair restor-
ers, weight-loss pills—that kind of stuff. Just calls a number and
punches in her code. As long as she has a phone and Internet, she's
got a job."

Bryce joined us and clicked off his flashlight. "Why would she
move to Red Rock? I hear Steamboat's really nice."

"That's a sad story. One of their nephews was visiting her in
Steamboat when he had an ATV accident. Rolled the thing on her
property after he hit a rock. Almost died. Still in the hospital with
brain damage."

CHAPTER 67

◑ *Bryce* ◑

Ashley hooked the leash on Bailey, and we headed back through the courtyard silently. Somehow, hearing that story made the world seem even colder. We'd thought so many negative things about Mr. Bookman and how he'd taken our ATV privileges away, but now it made sense.

The lightning and thunder had stopped, and a heavy white mist hung over us. Bailey was covered in mud and dirt and slobber. It was all we could do to drag him back through the slick grass. I held him at the back door while Ashley wiped his feet and coat with an old towel before we took him inside to his kennel.

The power was still off, and we'd left the candles burning by mistake. Leigh had predicted we'd burn the house down, and had we been out another half hour, she'd have been right.

"The whole robbery thing was probably just our imagination," I said, shaking my head. "I can't wait to hear from Boo about his talk with Mrs. Waldorf."

Ashley pulled a couple of toaster pastries from the freezer. "All this stuff is going to go bad soon."

"You gonna cook that by candlelight?"

She rolled her eyes. "I forgot again."

Right then the power came back. The TV news was just coming on, and the top story was about the fast-food robbery.

"The getaway car was spotted by a viewer in Red Rock not long after the initial reports," the news anchor said. "Let's go there live."

My mouth fell open. "So maybe it wasn't our imagination."

The reporter stood at an intersection in town near the on-ramp to the interstate, only a few blocks from the Prestons' house. The reporter wore a heavy coat, earmuffs, and gloves, and was shivering and spitting his words into the cold night air. "A viewer who saw our report was taking his children trick-or-treating when he saw an old car rumble through this intersection. Police are looking for a 1950s or 1960s Chevrolet, light in color, with license plates covered in mud."

They cut to a fast-food restaurant, where the owner said the robber had showed up after the big dinner rush. "Whoever it was got away with a lot of cash, but fortunately nobody was hurt."

The weather report said the strongest wave of storms had passed, but right behind it was another front that could bring more thunderstorms and even snow.

"Great," Ashley said. "I'm ready for this night to be over."

At that moment, the power went out again.

CHAPTER 68

✖ Ashley ✖

Bryce relit the candles, and I took the flashlight to check on the animals. As I passed the window, I noticed the lights in the other condos were on and the streetlights were lit.

"Weird," Bryce said. "Maybe our circuit breaker got turned off."

I followed him downstairs to the utility room.

Bryce opened the small gray door on the wall, revealing a bunch of switches. "I'm looking for one that's popped to the Off position. If something goes wrong with the electricity, a circuit gets tripped and shuts off."

"They all look fine to me."

We heard Bailey barking viciously and scratching at his kennel. We ran over there, pointing the flashlight all around. Bailey was going crazy, his kennel wobbling. "It's okay, boy. We're here now."

We went back upstairs. "Uh-oh," Bryce said, shining the light into the living room.

The front door was open.

CHAPTER 69

◕ *Bryce* ◕

We'd been set up. But by whom?

"Someone might be in the house, Ash," I whispered.

"Stop trying to scare me."

"I'm serious. They probably cut the power outside so they could get in without being seen."

"Let's get out of here."

We skipped and slid to Mrs. Waldorf's, only to find that her place was dark too.

"Did your lights just go off again?" I said.

She nodded, clearly terrified.

"Is there a central-power switch somewhere outside the house?" I said.

She thought a moment. "Now that you mention it, I think there is. When I moved in they gave me an orientation type of thing where they told me where everything was and what it did and all that." She squinted. "The fellow was younger and wore one of those handyman outfits—you know, with the tools on his belt. . . ."

All we needed was the location, not the entire story. "Uh, Mrs. Waldorf?"

She sighed. "I can't remember. Maybe that older man would know, the one in the condo by the garage."

CHAPTER 70

✖ Ashley ✖

Bryce and I saw Mr. Harper pass through his living room to the kitchen, so I rang the doorbell. We waited.

"Maybe you should try it again," Bryce said.

When I did, the light in the kitchen went out. Bryce shook his head and started down the steps.

Just then the door opened, and a disheveled Mr. Harper said, "Something wrong? You want to come in?"

"No. Our power is out, and the fish are gonna freeze if we don't get it back on. The circuit breaker in the house looks okay. Is there another one that controls both condos?"

His eyes widened. "As a matter of fact there is. In the garage. See that little door at the side? You want me to go in there with you?"

"I'm sure we can find it," I said.

"Well, I'm up. Let me just get my shoes."

When he came out he was surprised at the icy ground. "My clocks are messed up. The power must have gone out after I went to bed."

Then who was walking into the kitchen when we came up?

He fumbled with his keys and opened the small door. "I think yours is . . . yes, the middle one right here. Why, that's strange. The main breaker is off. Somebody would have to deliberately do that."

"Can you turn it back on for us?"

"Sure, but my goodness. I wonder . . ."

Bryce and I walked back toward the Prestons' condo. "Why didn't you tell him our suspicions?" I said.

"He could be involved."

"Involved with what?"

"I'm not sure, but somebody with a key to that door wanted to scare us."

With the lights on again, we agreed that we needed to give Bailey a bath (which is like bathing an SUV), because we wanted him out of his kennel and protecting us for the rest of the night.

I led him upstairs and found that the place had been trashed. Dresser drawers had been pulled out and emptied, clothes strewn about, beds turned over. In Binky's room, the same thing. In fact, most of the house had been ransacked, except the kitchen.

"Nothing's missing," Bryce said, "so they weren't stealing. They must have been looking for something or sending us a message."

"Like what?"

"I don't know," Bryce said. "But if they didn't find what they were looking for, they'll be back."

"Call the police."

"No, hang with me. We're going to figure this out. Let's get the dog clean and then start straightening up."

Bailey dug his claws into the floor tile and put his paws down, and I pulled while Bryce pushed. Then I ran the water while Bryce played hold-the-dog-by-the-collar. As soon as the tub was full, we had to pull and push him again, lifting his front paws.

When he finally got in and felt the warm water, it seemed to calm him. I did most of the bathing while Bryce kept looking out the door and down the stairs, listening for any movement.

"Bryce, somebody could still be here. Downstairs."

I dried Bailey as best I could, then had him search every room, closet, and bathroom. "I still say we should call the police," I said.

"What do we say? 'Someone messed up the house we're watching'?"

"We could tell them the old car might be here."

"We don't know that, and until we do, we should wait."

"I'm scared."

"Me too, Ash, but if we stick with this, we can figure it out."

CHAPTER 71

☺ *Bryce* ☺

Ashley camped out on the couch, and I stretched out by the patio door. If anybody came looking, I wanted to switch the lights on fast.

Bailey sat next to the couch licking his paws. That wet-dog smell wafted through the house. I wished there was a pet that could watch your stuff and not stink when it got wet or always have to go to the bathroom.

The clock by the stairs *tick, tick, tick*ed. After a while the sound irritated me until it was all I could think about.

Ashley whispered, "See anything out there?"

"No."

"You going to sleep?"

That meant she was getting tired and wanted permission, but she wasn't about to come right out and ask.

"You go ahead," I said. "I'll wake you up if I see anything."

"You sure?" she said, sounding exhausted.

I didn't even answer, and soon she was breathing heavily. I lay back and stared at the clock that glowed bluish green—11:44.

I watched every minute click by until 11:52. That's when I heard a flutter from upstairs. I froze, wondering if we'd locked the windows. The sound came again. Closer. Like it was near the top of the stairs.

"Ash?" I whispered. "You hear that?"

Bailey looked dead to the world, on his back, head against the couch and paws in the air.

Flutter. Flutter. Flutter.

Ping!

That sound came from the kitchen.

CHAPTER 72

❀ Ashley ❀

Something bounced off my forehead, and I sat up. Bailey's face was right next to mine, licking something from the blanket. Dog food. Little bits of dog food!

I sat up. "Why are you throwing—?"

"Shh!" Bryce said. "Something's in the house."

I held Bailey's jaw shut and heard a fluffy, fanning sound, then a ping. And another. I'd heard it before, but I couldn't place it.

I pushed the cover off and headed for the kitchen. The closer I got, the more familiar the sound became. I clicked on the flashlight, and there was Fred, gobbling the last bit of food in his cage.

"He's back!" I yelled, slamming the cage shut. "Can you believe it?"

Bryce took the flashlight and turned it off. "Yeah, that's great, but don't forget someone might be watching us."

I didn't care. The million-dollar bird was back. His food was down to almost nothing. He must have hidden somewhere in the house and flown to his cage to eat while Bryce and I were gone.

"Don't forget to feed the bird!" Fred said.

I clapped. "I want to call Mrs. Preston right now and have her talk to him."

"Hang on, Dr. Dolittle. We can talk to the animals later."

I poured bird food through the little slot outside Fred's cage, and some of it scattered on the floor. It didn't matter. We were going to have to clean the whole house before the Prestons returned anyway. A clean house and a full birdcage: two fewer reasons for the Prestons to want to kill us.

I remembered my dream of hearing the bird speak. It must not have been a dream. I'd heard Fred talking at night.

I lay back down on the couch, covered up, and stroked Bailey's ears. He gave a soft whimper and a moan and put his head on my knee. Bryce was still by the window. The moon had finally come out.

Then something moved near the patio.

CHAPTER 73

SATURDAY, NOVEMBER 1

☻ *Bryce* ☻

Ashley gasped like someone was about to pull her teeth out. I whirled to see a hulking form outside. My heart beat in my ears, and I couldn't breathe. I forced myself to take a deep breath and let it out.

The hulk stepped down from the rock ledge, jumped onto the concrete, and approached the glass door, peering inside. The latch on the door dipped slightly as the intruder tested it.

A low growl behind me told me that Bailey's earsplitting bark was coming.

I flicked on the light.

Whoever it was was a lot taller than me, wore a Bart Simpson mask, and carried a gun. You could have scraped me off the floor. Bailey erupted, causing Bart to jump the rock ledge and disappear into the night.

I was about to send Bailey to sic him when Ashley cried out, "He'll shoot Bailey! Don't let him out!"

We turned on all the lights in the house and sat, Ashley and I watching the patio door. Bailey, apparently exhausted from the excitement, fell fast asleep. Some guard dog.

"Should we call the police?" Ashley said. "Or Mom?"

"They guy's gone. He's not coming back." I said it with all the confidence I could muster, but we sat there all night, hardly blinking. Every half hour or so, Fred would say something and Ashley would jump. I finally threw a towel over his cage, and that shut him up.

When the sun came up, Ashley and I vacuumed, dusted, made beds, washed dishes, and got the house cleaner than when the Prestons left.

By 8:30 the place was sparkling except for a full trash bag. I packed it tight and tied the top, then found the garage-door opener.

Someone had thrown eggs at all the garage doors. A trick because of no treat?

Mr. Harper came out, and when he saw the egg mess, he shook his head. "It's a shame what kids will do these days," he said, punching his garage opener. "I see you survived the power problem."

I nodded. "Where are you headed?"

"Church. That's another thing my wife and I used to do. They have a breakfast every Saturday."

I'd seen hypocrites before, people who say they're Christians but act the opposite. Mr. Harper was still a suspect as far as I was concerned. An old Volkswagen Beetle was parked in his first stall. Beside it sat another car with a cover over it.

"What's under there?" I said.

Mr. Harper smiled. "A 1955 Chevy Bel Air. First year they made 'em. Want to see it?"

He pulled the cover off, revealing a gleaming white car that looked straight out of a 1950s movie.

"Have a nice breakfast," I said, and he drove off in his Beetle.

PART 5

CHAPTER 74

❀ Ashley ❀

"It fits the description perfectly," Bryce said. "But why would Mr. Harper let me see it? He's gotta know we suspect him."

We took Bailey out for a walk and ran into Tyler. He seemed a lot better. "What do you know about Mr. Harper?" I said.

He shrugged. "Keeps to himself a lot. I was here when they moved him and his son into the place, but I haven't—"

"He has a son?" Bryce said.

Tyler nodded. "In a wheelchair. They had to get four guys to carry him up the steps."

"What's wrong with him?" I said.

"Some kind of accident. My mom said he might get better and be able to walk, but something happened to his throat and he'll never be able to talk. Just wheezes and rasps."

As we headed back in, the pieces were starting to come together—pieces we hadn't even known were there. But one thing still bothered us.

"If Mr. Harper's son is the holdup guy, what does he want in our condo?"

Bryce shrugged.

"Now we should call the police," I said. "We know where the car is. They can put it together from there."

Bryce nodded.

I headed for the kitchen phone. That's when I saw a man standing by the fridge, waving a gun. He had pale skin, curly hair that stuck out at all different angles, a wide nose, a half-shaven face, and dark circles under his eyes. Blue eyes. Deep blue.

He put a hand to his throat and told Bryce, "Leave the dog outside." It was more of a rasp than a voice, but we understood him.

Bryce closed the door, hooking the leash to the outside handle so Bailey wouldn't get away.

"Lock it," the man said. Bryce did. "What did you do with it?"

I looked at Bryce, then back at the man. "With what?"

He took a step forward. "You know. Where is it?"

"Mister," Bryce said, "we don't know what you're talking about."

The man gritted his teeth. "The money. You dug it up from my backyard. Now where did you put it?"

Someone knocked at the front door, and the man's eyes grew wide.

"Ashley? Bryce? You in there?"

"It's Mrs. Waldorf from next door," I said. "She'll be upset if we don't answer."

He waved his gun. "Get rid of her. And remember, I have your brother in here."

I opened the door, and Mrs. Waldorf eyed me suspiciously. "I heard Bailey barking. Is everything all right?"

"Yeah, we just wanted to give him some fresh air." I reached in my pocket and felt the piece of paper I had stashed earlier with the number of the police from the newscast.

"Have the Prestons told you when they'll be back?" she said.

"It's supposed to be tomorrow." I shoved the paper into her hand. "The funeral was yesterday. Just call this number and you can reach them. Thanks for checking on us."

CHAPTER 75

☺ *Bryce* ☺

"She's gone," Ashley said.

"Good," the man rasped. "Now take me to the money."

"Your dad is so nice," Ashley said. "Why do you want to do something like this?"

I knew she was trying to stall, but the guy's face told me he was at the breaking point. He wanted his money. Problem was, we didn't have it.

"I can take you to it, but we have to go outside," Ashley said.

"Where outside?" the man said. Every time he talked, he had to hold his hand to his throat.

"In the courtyard. Right out there."

He looked out the window. "Get that dog in his kennel. If he comes at me, I'll shoot him."

Ashley opened the door and pulled Bailey inside. I got him into his kennel.

"Follow me," Ashley said.

The phone rang as we were going out. The man closed the door behind him and waved us on.

"What are you doing?" I whispered.

"I think Bailey dug up this guy's money and hid it somewhere."

Ashley led us to where Boo and Mrs. Waldorf had spoken the night before. All around the courtyard lay little mounds of dirt where Bailey had dug something up. This spot was covered, but not by hands. Bailey's paw prints were all around.

"Dig it up," the man said.

Ashley and I dug with our fingers and scraped dirt from the hole. It didn't take long to reach the first plastic bag. It was fogged up and mud caked. There was black and brown and red stuff inside, and the whole thing felt stiff.

"This isn't it, is it?" I said.

"No."

We dug some more. Out came another of Mrs. Waldorf's plastic bags. We laid it atop the other and kept going. We retrieved four bags before I hit something solid and cut my finger.

I cleared the dirt from the top of a metal box. The handle still had drool on it, so that must have been how Bailey had carried it. The box wasn't huge, but it was heavy. I set it on the ground beside the man.

He opened it. Wads of cash were stuffed inside a rubber mask. He slammed it shut and latched it.

That's when I heard a siren. The man cursed, left us in the dirt, and ran toward the garage. He was halfway there when he stopped and turned around. The word *hostage* flashed through my mind, and I grabbed Ashley's arm.

"Over here!" Mrs. Waldorf yelled.

We ducked inside her house, and the man turned again. Just as he got to the garage, police cars screeched and people yelled. Soon a crowd in pajamas stood gawking at this guy being led away with his hands cuffed behind his back. The '55 Bel Air seemed to just sit there watching the whole thing with its big headlights.

Mr. Bookman stood nearby in a checkered robe, and as Ashley and I approached, he said, "What have you two been doing? You're filthy!"

Back at Mrs. Waldorf's place the police took our statements.

CHAPTER 76

❀ Ashley ❀

Mr. Harper had no idea that his son was stealing stuff. He didn't even know the boy could get out of his wheelchair. While Mr. Harper was out, his son had pulled off the robberies, using his father's classic car.

The police found hundreds of clips from movies on the son's computer. That's how he had recorded dialogue to use in the robberies. They also found a digital recorder hooked to a big speaker inside the Chevy's glove compartment.

We asked what was in those plastic bags Bailey had dug up, and Mrs. Waldorf blushed. "I can't believe that dog would dig up my precious ones."

"Precious ones?" Bryce said.

"Every living being is precious, I think. It hurts so much when I'm driving and I see one of them at the side of the road."

"Roadkill?" I said. *No wonder Boo ran away.*

She smiled. "Each deserves a decent burial, not to be left out there alone. So I bring them back here and say a few words and let them go to their rest."

"That's admirable," Mr. Harper said.

That's sick, I thought.

"It's good to know there are still people in the world who take the time to care for things," Mr. Harper said.

The Prestons arrived home late the next afternoon. Mrs. Preston tried to act like the dead fish and the forgotten trash didn't matter, but I knew better. They were impressed by how clean the house was—except for the curtain rod in their room, where we found out Fred had hidden—and how healthy the other animals seemed. Bailey couldn't stop licking their hands and wagging his tail.

Mrs. Preston said I shouldn't have stressed out over Binky's feeding. "He can go months without a rat if he has to."

I looked at Bryce and just shook my head.

I told Mrs. Preston everything that had gone on, and I think she thought I was making the whole thing up, until Mrs. Waldorf came and told her the same story.

"Well, you certainly have been busy," Mrs. Preston said.

A lot busier than we wanted to be.

CHAPTER 77

☺ *Bryce* ☺

Leigh and Sam got home from their trip late Sunday night, and all Leigh could talk about was how beautiful the college was, what the dorms were like, blah, blah, blah.

Sam listened to our story, raising his eyebrows when he heard about the gun and the stolen money, and shaking his head and smiling at the rest.

"You thought the dad was alone in his condo," he said.

"We just assumed," I said.

"His son had been in trouble before, so his dad said he could stay there until he recovered from his injury," Ashley said. "I think

Mr. Harper was a little ashamed of him and thought he'd be moving out."

"Why did the son hide the money?" Sam said.

"So his dad wouldn't find it," I said. "Mr. Harper came to his room every couple of days looking for cigarettes and stuff, so he knew he had to hide the money outside."

Sam shook his head. "Wonder what he was saving up for."

"We may never know," I said. "But the police said he had more than $25,000 in that metal box."

When Ashley and I got home from school the next day there was a check from Mrs. Preston on the kitchen blackboard.

We figured out that, minus the money we'd paid for the extra rat and the locksmith, Ashley and I had made $3. That meant $1.50 each. Not even enough to go to a movie.

Leigh saw us staring at the check. "Told you."

But you can't put a price tag on a solved crime. Burger Barn gave us coupons for a bunch of free dinners. The same happened with the restaurants in Colorado Springs.

We ordered Super Burgers and had Mom drive us to the Prestons' so we could give Bailey part of our reward. It was only fair.

On the way home I spotted a dead raccoon at the side of the road. Mrs. Waldorf and Mr. Harper would probably be holding a burial service that night.

About the Authors

Jerry B. Jenkins (jerryjenkins.com) is the writer of the Left Behind series. He owns the Jerry B. Jenkins Christian Writers Guild, an organization dedicated to mentoring aspiring authors. Former vice president for publishing for the Moody Bible Institute of Chicago, he also served many years as editor of *Moody* magazine and is now Moody's writer-at-large.

His writing has appeared in publications as varied as *Reader's Digest, Parade, Guideposts*, in-flight magazines, and dozens of other periodicals. Jenkins's biographies include books with Billy Graham, Hank Aaron, Bill Gaither, Luis Palau, Walter Payton, Orel Hershiser, and Nolan Ryan, among many others. His books appear regularly on the *New York Times, USA Today, Wall Street Journal*, and *Publishers Weekly* best-seller lists.

Jerry is also the writer of the nationally syndicated sports story comic strip *Gil Thorp,* distributed to newspapers across the United States by Tribune Media Services.

Jerry and his wife, Dianna, live in Colorado and have three grown sons and three grandchildren.

Chris Fabry is a writer and broadcaster who lives in Colorado. He has written more than 40 books, including collaboration on the Left Behind: The Kids series.

You may have heard his voice on Focus on the Family, Moody Broadcasting, or Love Worth Finding. He has also written for Adventures in Odyssey and Radio Theatre.

Chris is a graduate of the W. Page Pitt School of Journalism at Marshall University in Huntington, West Virginia. He and his wife, Andrea, have been married 23 years and have nine children, a bird, two dogs, and one cat.

RED ROCK MYSTERIES

The first 12 books now available:

#1 Haunted Waters

#2 Stolen Secrets

#3 Missing Pieces

#4 Wild Rescue

#5 Grave Shadows

#6 Phantom Writer

#7 Double Fault

#8 Canyon Echoes

#9 Instant Menace

#10 Escaping Darkness

#11 Windy City Danger

#12 Hollywood Holdup

**WATCH FOR THE NEXT 4 BOOKS
COMING SEPTEMBER 2006!**

WheRe
AdvEnture
beGins
with
a BoOk!

∠LoG oN @
Cool2Read.com